AUTHOR	CLASS
PERUTZ, L	F — G

TITLE The Marquis of Bolibar

THE MARQUIS OF BOLIBAR

THE MARQUIS OF BOLIBAR

Leo Perutz

Translated from the German
by John Brownjohn

COLLINS HARVILL
8 Grafton Street, London W1
1989

COLLINS HARVILL
William Collins Sons & Co. Ltd
London · Glasgow · Sydney · Auckland
Toronto · Johannesburg

BRITISH LIBRARY CATALOGUING IN PUBLICATION DATA

Perutz, Leo
[Der Marques de Bolibar, *English*] The
marquis of Bolibar.
I. Title   II. Brownjohn (J. Maxwell),
John Maxwell, *1929*–
838'.9'1209

ISBN 0-00-271514-7

Published in Austria by Paul Zsolnay Verlag, Vienna
under the title *Der Marques de Bolibar*

Originally published in Great Britain 1926
This edition published in Great Britain
by Collins Harvill 1989

© Paul Zsolnay Verlag G.m.b.H., Vienna, Hamburg 1960
English translation © William Collins Sons & Co. Ltd 1989

Photoset in Linotron Bembo by
Rowland Phototypesetting Ltd, Bury St Edmunds, Suffolk
Printed and bound in Great Britain by
Hartnolls Ltd, Bodmin, Cornwall

CONTENTS

Foreword   vii

A Morning Walk   1
The Tanner's Tub   11
Three Signals   22
Snow on the Roofs   28
Captain de Salignac   37
The Coming of God   42
German Serenade   55
Trounced   66
With Saul to Endor   82
A Forgathering of Saints   97
The Song of Talavera   111
Fire   122
A Prayer   128
The Courier   141
Insurrection   147
The Blue Buttercup   153
The Final Signal   162
Catastrophe   170
The Marquis of Bolibar   177

FOREWORD

The death of Eduard von Jochberg occurred at Dillenburg, a small town in the former Duchy of Nassau, not long before the outbreak of the Franco-Prussian War. An eccentric and almost pathologically uncommunicative old gentleman, he spent most of each year on his country estate. It was only toward the end of his life, when his health began to fail, that he moved to the little market town for good.

None of Herr von Jochberg's few close acquaintances – horses and hounds were his principal companions – knew that he was an old soldier who had, in his youth, participated in some of Napoleon I's campaigns. No one had ever heard him allude to his experiences during this period of his life, far less describe them in detail. Those who had known him were all the more surprised, therefore, when his personal effects yielded a bundle of manuscript, neatly tied and sealed, which proved on closer scrutiny to be his recollections of the Peninsular War.

This unexpected find caused a considerable stir throughout the province of Nassau and in the adjoining Grand Duchy of Hesse. Articles on Herr von Jochberg's memoirs appeared in the local press, together with long excerpts therefrom; scholars of repute inspected them; and the dead man's heirs – his nephew Wilhelm von Jochberg, a lecturer at Bonn University, and an elderly lady from Aachen named Fräulein von Hartung – were bombarded with offers by publishers. In short, Herr von Jochberg's memoirs were on everyone's lips, and even the war, which broke out soon afterwards, proved insufficient to dispel all public interest in them.

Why? Because they dealt with an obscure and hitherto unexplained chapter in German military history: the annihilation by Spanish guerrillas of two local regiments, the Nassau and the Prince of Hesse's Own.

Little information about this episode in the Spanish campaign can be gleaned from the literature on the subject. August Scherbruch, a captain in the service of the Grand Duchy of Hesse and a noted military historian of the Napoleonic era, devotes only two-and-a-half lines to "the tragedy of La Bisbal" in *Der Kampf auf der Pyrenäischen Halbinsel, 1807–1813*, a six-volume work published by Langermann of Halle. Stranger still, Dr Hermann Schwartze, a Darmstadt historian who published an extremely painstaking account of the part played in Napoleon I's campaigns by Hessian troops, makes no reference whatever to the fact that two regiments belonging to the Confederation of the Rhine were wiped out to a man. It also escapes mention in the less comprehensive works by Kraus, Leistikov, and Fischer-Tübingen. A critical study entitled *Die Rheinbundtruppen in Spanien. Ein Beitrag zur Strategie der Unvernunft* (Karlsruhe 1826) and published anonymously, doubtless by an officer discharged from the forces of Baden, is the only one to deal at length with "the catastrophe of La Bisbal", but without contributing any details of moment. It does, however, identify the officer commanding both regiments as Colonel von Leslie, a name that recurs in Lieutenant von Jochberg's memoirs.

Not unnaturally, somewhat fuller accounts are given by the opposing side. Among the major works available to me I would cite that by Don Silvio Gaeta, a colonel on the Spanish General Staff, who concludes that the defeat of the German troops at La Bisbal represented a definite turning point in the course of the campaign and crucially affected General Cuesta's further operations. Simon Ventura, an apothecary who, in addition to a life of Santa Maria de'Pazzi, a *Handbook for Amateurs of Fungi* and *The Tulip Festival*, a tragedy rather too turgid in style for the modern taste, wrote a history of his native La Bisbal, displays a largely accurate but purely superficial knowledge of the course of events. Pedro Orosco, too, mentions the destruction of the two regiments in *Los jefers de la guerilla en las Asturias*, a work of which I possess one of the few extant copies, though his account teems with glaring errors and inaccuracies.

All in all, however, these and other Spanish historical works do little or nothing to explain the astonishing fact that both German regiments vanished without trace. Lieutenant von Jochberg's literary remains alone shed light on the strange events that ultimately conduced to the tragedy at La Bisbal.

If Jochberg's account is correct, it presents us with a phenomenon unique in the annals of military history: *the annihilation of the Nassau Regiment was directly occasioned – indeed, almost deliberately engineered – by its own officers!* Despite the modern tendency to enlist explanations of an occult and mystical nature, not to mention concepts such as the "death wish" or autosuggestion, one finds this hard to credit. Professional historians will doubtless take a sceptical view of Lieutenant von Jochberg's memoirs and dismiss them as unduly fanciful. Far be it from me to censure them on that account. After all, how great a critical faculty can one attribute to a man who became convinced that one of the persons he encountered in Spain was the legendary Wandering Jew?

Lieutenant von Jochberg's reminiscences have been abridged to some two-thirds of their original length. Many passages not directly relevant to the subject – an account of the fighting at Talavera and Torres Vedras, a description of the so-called "stick dance" at La Bisbal, sundry digressions and conversations of a political, philosophical and literary nature, an appreciation of the art treasures in La Bisbal's town hall, and a long-winded exposition of the genealogical ties between Jochberg's family and that of Captain Count Schenk zu Castel-Borckenstein – all these have fallen prey to the editor's pencil. While denying the reader much that is of historical interest, this has enhanced the narrative's impact and inherent suspense.

And now let Lieutenant von Jochberg himself recount the singular experiences he underwent at La Bisbal, a town in the Asturian highlands, during the winter of 1812.

A MORNING WALK

It was eight in the morning when we at last sighted the two white church towers of La Bisbal. We were soaked to the skin, I and my fifteen dragoons and Captain von Eglofstein, the regimental adjutant, who had come to negotiate with the *alcalde*, or mayor of the town.

Our regiment had, the previous day, survived a fierce encounter with the guerrillas under their Colonel Saracho, whom our men for some reason unknown to me – perhaps on account of his corpulent figure – called the "Tanner's Tub". Having succeeded toward nightfall in scattering the rebels, we pursued them into their forests and very nearly captured Saracho himself, for he suffered from gout and could move but slowly on foot.

Thereafter we bivouacked in open country, much to the chagrin of my dragoons, who cursed their inability even to obtain some dry straw on which to sleep after such a day's exertions. I jokingly promised each of them a feather bed with silken curtains once we reached La Bisbal, and they professed themselves content.

I myself spent a part of the night with Eglofstein and Donop in the colonel's quarters. We drank mulled wine and played faro, hoping to cheer him, but he so persisted in talking of his late wife that we had to put down our cards and listen – and it was all we could do not to give ourselves away, for there was no officer in the whole of the Nassau Regiment whose mistress Françoise-Marie had not at some time been.

I set out with Eglofstein and my dragoons at five in the morning. *"Prenez garde des guérillas!"* the colonel called after

I

me as I rode off. It was a task that properly belonged to the officer of the day, but, being the most junior subaltern in the regiment, I had no choice.

The road was clear and the insurgents gave us no trouble. A few dead mules lay in our path. Just outside the village of Figueras we came upon two dead Spaniards who had dragged themselves thus far in a moribund condition. One was a guerrilla belonging to Saracho's band, the other wore the uniform of the Numancia Regiment. They must have been hoping to reach the village under cover of darkness when death overtook them.

Figueras itself we found entirely deserted by its inhabitants, the peasants having fled into the mountains with their herds of sheep. Three or four Spaniards – *dispersos*, or stragglers cut off from Saracho's main force – were sitting in a tavern on the outskirts of the village, but they hurriedly made off at our approach. They yelled "*Muerte a los Franceses!*" like madmen as soon as they reached the edge of the forest, but none of them fired a shot. "For ever and ever, amen, you he-goats!" Such was the shouted response of one of my dragoons, Corporal Thiele, who thought – God alone knows why – that "*Muerte a los Franceses*" signified "Praise the Lord Jesus" in German.

On reaching our destination we found the alcalde awaiting us outside the town gate with the entire junta and several other citizens. He stepped forward as we dismounted and greeted us with the words that were customary on such occasions. La Bisbal, he assured us, was well-disposed toward the French because Colonel Saracho's guerrillas had done its citizens much harm, looted their property, and driven off the peasants' cattle. Such ill-disposed people as had settled in the town were very few. He begged us to be merciful, for he and his fellow citizens were eager to do all in their power to assist the gallant soldiers of the great Napoleon. Eglofstein curtly replied that he himself could promise nothing: the colonel's decision alone would determine what treatment the town could expect. He then accompanied the alcalde and his clerk to the town hall to have the billeting warrants made out. The townsfolk who had mutely and apprehensively witnessed this conversation, hat in hand, dispersed and hurried home to their wives.

Having posted some of my men at the gate, I repaired to a roadside *posada* or inn beyond the walls, there to await the arrival of the regiment over a cup of hot chocolate, which the landlord produced with alacrity.

After breakfast I went out into the garden, for the air in the cramped little tap-room stank of boiled fish and had made me queasy. The garden was neither large nor well-tended, the landlord having planted it at random with onions and garlic, pumpkins and broad beans, but the scent of the rain-sodden soil did me good. Moreover, the garden adjoined a spacious park in which grew fig trees, elms, and walnut trees. A narrow footpath flanked by yew hedges led between expanses of grass to a pool, and in the background stood a white-walled country house whose slate roof, wet with rain, I had earlier glimpsed from the road.

My corporal followed me out of the tap-room and into the garden. Exceedingly annoyed, he strode up to me with a reproachful air.

"Lieutenant!" he cried. "Musty flour in our breakfast gruel, soup at midday, and bread and garlic for supper – such has been our fare for weeks now, yet when one of us stopped a peasant on the road and requisitioned an egg or two, he was brought before a court martial. Tables laden with food, the best wine put to cool, and a goodly piece of bacon in every cook-pot – that was what you promised us when we reached La Bisbal, and now . . ."

"Well? What did the landlord serve you?"

"Rotten little pincer-fish, twelve for a groschen!" the corporal cried angrily, and thrust his hand under my nose. On it reposed a small shrimp such as Spanish peasants steep in jugs of vinegar.

"Come now, Thiele," I replied in jocular vein, "the Bible tells us that God gave man everything that moveth and liveth to be for his meat, so why not that shrimp?"

The corporal opened his mouth to remonstrate, but no adequate rejoinder to my Biblical quotation occurred to him.

3

A moment later he put a finger to his lips and gripped me by the wrist. He had seen something that made him forget his ill-temper in an instant.

"Lieutenant," he said softly, "there's someone hiding over yonder."

I dropped to the ground in a trice and crawled stealthily toward the garden fence.

"One of the guerrillas," the corporal whispered close beside me, "– there, under that bush.'

Sure enough, I saw a man crouching among the laurel bushes barely ten paces from me. He carried neither sword nor musket; if he was armed, he must have had his weapons concealed beneath his clothes.

"There's another – and another, and another! There must be more than a dozen of them, Lieutenant. What devil's work can they be up to?"

I could make out more men lying or crouching everywhere – behind the trunks of the elms and walnut trees, in the yew hedges, in the bushes, on the grass. As yet, none of them appeared to have seen us.

"I'll hurry back to the inn and warn the others," whispered the corporal. "This must be the guerrillas' lair or headquarters. The Tanner's Tub cannot be far away."

Just then a tall old man in a dark cloak trimmed with velvet came out of the house and slowly descended the steps, head bowed.

"They're after him, I'll wager," I said softly, and drew my pistol.

"The bandits plan to murder him!" hissed the corporal.

"When I vault the fence," I told him, "follow me and have at them." No sooner had I spoken than a figure rose from the lee of a mound of gravel and ran up behind the old man.

I raised the pistol and took aim, only to lower it a moment later, for then we witnessed the strangest occurrence I ever saw in my life. One of my mother's brothers is a physician to a lunatic asylum at Kissingen – I used to visit him on occasion as a boy – and in truth, I now fancied myself transported to the garden of that same madhouse. One pace to the old man's

4

rear the fellow came to a halt, doffed his cap, and addressed him at the top of his voice.

"Greetings, Señor Marques de Bolibar! A very good morning to Your Excellency!"

The same instant, a lanky, bald-headed fellow in muleteer's garb darted out from behind a sandstone statue. He, too, pranced clumsily up to the old man, halted, and bowed low.

"My respects, Señor Marques. May you live a thousand years."

But the strangest thing of all was that the old man continued on his way as if he had neither seen nor heard the pair of them. I could discern his face, now that he was closer to me, and inordinately stiff and motionless it looked. His locks were snow-white, his brow and cheeks pale, his eyes lowered. As for his bold and terrible cast of feature, I shall never forget it.

While he walked on, the other men deserted their places of concealment one by one. Like figures in a puppet show they popped out of bushes, emerged from behind tree trunks and under garden benches, jumped down from trees, and, placing themselves in his path, accosted him.

"Your most obedient servant, Señor Marques de Bolibar!"

"Good day, Señor Marques. How fares Your Grace?"

"My humblest respects, Your Honour!"

But the nobleman threaded his way in silence through the lackeys who swarmed around him like flies around a dish of honey. He made no attempt to fend off their importunities. His face was as unmoved as if all these noisy salutations were directed, not at him, but at some other person invisible to me.

While the corporal and I were gazing open-mouthed at this curious spectacle, a shaggy little fellow darted out of a summerhouse and minced up to the old man in the manner of a dancing master. Having halted, he busily scratched at the ground with his feet like a hen on a dunghill and addressed him in execrable French.

"If it isn't my friend Bolibar! Delighted to see you!"

But not even he, who behaved as if they were the best of friends, attracted a single glance. A lone figure lost in thought, or so it seemed, the old nobleman returned to his house, climbed the steps, and, as silently as he had come, vanished into the gloomy interior.

We rose to our feet and watched while the servants, arm in arm now, followed their master into the house in small groups, chatting and smoking as they went.

"Well," I said to the corporal, "what the devil was all that about?"

He thought awhile. Then he said, "These Spanish grandees are dignified beyond measure and melancholy in the extreme. It's in their nature to be so."

"The Marquis of Bolibar must be a perfect idiot, so his servants treat him as such and make sport of him. Come, let's return to the tap-room. The landlord will be able to tell us why the Marquis's gardeners, coachmen, grooms and lackeys greeted him with such ceremony, and why they earned no thanks for it."

"They were celebrating his name-day, I'll be bound," said the corporal. "If you wish to return to the tap-room, Lieutenant, do so alone. I would sooner remain outside than venture back into that rat's nest. The tablecloth is as tattered as our regimental colours after the battle of Talavera, and the landlord's floor is covered with dung enough to dress every Spanish field between Pamplona and Malaga."

He lingered outside the door while I betook myself to the proprietor of the posada, who was busy frying thin slices of bread in oil. His wife was lying on the floor and fanning the flames with the aid of a makeshift bellows, the tube being an old musket barrel.

"Who owns the big house over yonder?" I asked.

"A nobleman," replied the landlord, without looking up from his work. "The wealthiest man in the entire province."

"I can well believe that such a mansion wasn't built to house geese or goats," I said. "How does the owner style himself?"

The landlord eyed me warily. "His Excellency the noble Señor Marques de Bolibar," he said at length.

"The Marquis of Bolibar," I mused. "A haughty gentleman, no doubt, and unduly jealous of his rank."

"Not at all! An affable and kindly soul, for all his noble birth

— a truly devout Christian and far from haughty. No matter who salutes him in the street, be it a water-carrier or the Reverend Father himself, he returns their greetings with equal friendliness."

"But he's somewhat weak in the head, surely?" I hazarded a lie to draw him out. "Urchins run after him in the street, I'm told. They taunt and tease him by calling his name aloud."

"What!" the landlord exclaimed with a look of surprise and consternation. "Who could have fed you such untruth, Señor caballero? There isn't a wiser man in all the province, believe me. Peasants from every village in the neighbourhood make pilgrimage to him when they don't know where to turn on account of their cattle, or their wives, or the high taxes."

The landlord's words seemed quite out of tune with the scene I had just witnessed in the garden, and again I had a vision of the old man as he walked, mute and expressionless, through that noisy, chattering throng of servants, making no attempt to shoo them away. I was just debating whether to tell the landlord precisely what I had seen from his garden when my ears were assailed by a blare of trumpets and a clatter of hoofs. Hearing the colonel's voice, I hurried out into the street.

My regiment had arrived. The grenadiers, begrimed and streaked with sweat after their hours-long march, had fallen out and were sitting by the roadside to left and right. The officers dismounted and called for their servants. I went up to the colonel and presented my report.

The colonel listened to me with only half an ear. He was studying the terrain and wondering how best to improve the fortifications. In his mind's eye he was already constructing ramparts and bastions, mines and redoubts for the defence of the town.

Captain Brockendorf and several other officers were standing beside the ox cart laden with their valises. I joined him and described the Marquis of Bolibar's curious morning promenade. He listened with an air of disbelief, shaking his head the while, but Lieutenant Günther, who was seated beside him on an upturned bucket, had an explanation ready.

"Many of these Spanish grandees are the queerest fish imaginable. They never tire of hearing their fine-sounding names, which are so long that you could say three whole rosaries in the time it takes to recite them. It delights them to hear their servants reel off their titles in full, all day long. At Salamanca, when I was billeted on the Conde de Veyra . . . ."

He launched into an account of his experiences in the household of that proud Spanish nobleman, but Lieutenant Donop cut him short.

"Bolibar? Did you say Bolibar? Why, that was the name of our late lamented Marquesin!"

"Yes indeed," cried Brockendorf, "you're right. What's more, he once told me that his family owned an estate in the neighbourhood of La Bisbal."

A young Spanish nobleman had served in our regiment as a volunteer – one of the few of his nation to have been so fired with the ideals of liberty and justice that he espoused the cause of France and the Emperor. He was estranged from his family and had disclosed his true name and provenance to two or three of his comrades only, but the Spanish peasants called him "el Marquesin" – for he was short and slight of stature – and we, too, addressed him by that sobriquet. Having fallen in battle with the guerrillas the previous night, he now lay buried in the village graveyard at Bascaras.

"That settles it," said Donop. "Your Marquis of Bolibar, Jochberg, is a kinsman of our Marquesin. It behoves us to inform the old man, as gently and considerately as possible, of our gallant comrade's death. Since you're already acquainted with the Marquis, Jochberg, will you take it upon yourself to do so?"

I saluted and made my way to the nobleman's house with one of my men, meanwhile rehearsing the words with which I proposed to fulfil my difficult and thankless task.

A wall lay between the house and the road, but it had crumbled away at so many points that one could easily get across. As I neared the building I was met by a babble of loud, plaintive, quarrelsome voices. I knocked on the door, and the din ceased at once.

"Who's there?" called a voice.

"I come in peace," I replied.

"Who comes in peace?"

"A German officer."

"*Ave Maria purissima!*" wailed someone. "It isn't he!" The door was opened and I walked in.

I found myself in a vestibule where lackeys, coachmen, gardeners and other servants were running hither and thither in great dismay and confusion. The shaggy little fellow who had addressed the Marquis as "my friend" was also present. He minced up to me in his dancing master's fashion, puce in the face with agitation, and introduced himself as His Grace the Marquis's steward and majordomo.

"I wish to speak with the Marquis in person," I told him.

The majordomo clasped his head with both hands, breathing heavily.

"The Señor Marques?" he groaned. "O merciful God, merciful God!" He stared at me awhile. Then he said, "Alas, Lieutenant or Captain or whatever you may be, His Grace isn't here."

"How so, not here?" I said sternly. "I myself saw him in his garden earlier this morning."

"Earlier this morning, perhaps, but now he's gone." The majordomo turned and called to a man who was hurrying through the vestibule.

"Pasqual! Have you looked in the stables? Is none of the horses missing?"

"None, Señor Fabricio. They're all accounted for."

"The saddle horses too? Capitan the grey and San Miguel the roan? What of Hermosa the mare – is she also in her stall?"

"They're all there," the groom repeated. "Not one is missing."

"Then may God, the Virgin and all the Saints assist us. Our master has vanished – he must have met with an accident."

"When did you see him last?" I asked.

"Not half an hour ago, in his bedchamber. He was standing before the mirror, looking at himself. He had instructed me to burst into the room, time and again, and inquire after his health. 'Did Your Grace pass a restful night?' I had to ask, or, as if I

9

were one of his friends from Madrid, 'Heaven bless you, Bolibar, what are *you* doing here?' I had to repeat that several times while he stood before the mirror and studied his reflection."

"And this morning in the garden?"

"The Señor Marques behaved strangely all morning. He made us hide in the bushes and call his name aloud. God alone knows what he had in mind, but our master never does anything without an excellent reason."

At that point the gardener entered with his lad. The majordomo promptly abandoned me and flew at him.

"What are you waiting for? Drain the pool at once, do you hear?" Then, turning to me, he sighed and said, "God grant we may give him an honourable Christian burial if we find him at the bottom of the pool . . ."

I left the house and told my comrades what I had heard. We were still discussing the matter when a wounded officer was carried past on a litter.

"Bolibar?" he exclaimed suddenly. "Who spoke that name?"

Although he wore the uniform of another regiment, I knew him. The wounded officer was Lieutenant von Rohn of the Hanoverian Chasseurs, with whom I had shared quarters for two weeks the previous summer. He had been shot through the chest.

"I did," I said. "What of the Marquis of Bolibar? Do you know him?"

He gazed at me in horror, his eyes glittering with fever.

"Seize him quickly," he cried in a hoarse voice, "or he'll destroy you all."

THE TANNER'S TUB

Lieutenant von Rohn succumbed to the effects of his wound two days later in the Convent of Santa Engracia, which we fitted out as a hospital immediately after our arrival in La Bisbal. During this time he was repeatedly questioned by our colonel and Captain Eglofstein about the details of his encounter with Colonel Saracho and the Marquis of Bolibar. Although he was not always fully conscious, his statements gave us a sufficient knowledge of what had been agreed that night – the night after our skirmish with the guerrillas – between the Marquis of Bolibar, the "Tanner's Tub" and Captain William O'Callaghan of the British Army. His account of what happened at St Rochus' chapel in the woods of Bascaras enlightened us on the nature and abilities of the Marquis of Bolibar, and on what to expect from that dangerous foe of France and the Emperor.

Lieutenant von Rohn's regimental commander had dispatched him to Marshal Soult's headquarters at Forgosa with some important papers, to wit, the *feuilles d'appel* or muster rolls of the Hanoverian Chasseurs, because the assistant paymaster had refused to disburse any monies without them. The area between Marshal Soult's Fourth Corps and General d'Hilliers' brigade, to which the Hanoverian Chasseurs belonged, was temporarily controlled by the insurgents who also held La Bisbal and its environs, so Lieutenant von Rohn was compelled to avoid the more convenient highroad and use the winding forest tracks that led through the mountains to Forgosa.

At this stage in his account Lieutenant von Rohn inveighed

bitterly against the army's book-keepers. He wished he could dig all the quartermasters and planners and pen-pushers out of their comfortable chairs at headquarters and transplant them to the rugged Spanish highlands; *that* would soon teach them to treat honest soldiers in a fitting manner. His regiment was always short of something, be it boots or cartridges, and they had once been obliged to use garden tubs instead of gabions. Here he went off at a tangent and began to speak of pay, fiercely complaining that a lieutenant earned twenty-two thalers a month at home but only eighteen on campaign. "Junot is insane!" he cried, half delirious with fever. "How can an utter lunatic continue to command an army corps! He's a brave man, mark you. In battle he has been known to borrow a private soldier's musket and blaze away . . ."

Eglofstein broke in with a question, whereupon the lieutenant grew calmer and returned to the subject in hand.

On the evening of the second day he traversed the wood near Bascaras escorted by his soldier servant. While picking their way through the dense undergrowth – their horses were more of a hindrance than a help in such difficult terrain – they heard musket-fire and the din of the battle in progress between us and the guerrillas on the highroad not far away. Rohn at once changed direction and set off uphill, seeking safety in the recesses of the wood. A few minutes later he was hit in the chest by a stray bullet. He fell to the ground and briefly lost consciousness.

On regaining his senses he found that the servant had lashed him to his saddle with two thongs. They had almost reached the summit of the hill, but the din of battle was far louder than before. Individual voices and words of command could now be distinguished, together with oaths and the cries of wounded men.

In a clearing on the brow of the hill stood a ruined chapel once dedicated to St Rochus but now employed as a barn. Here the servant reined in, for the wounded lieutenant had lost so much blood that he feared he would die on him. They would be bound to fall into the Spaniards' hands unless something were done quickly, he said, so he lifted the lieutenant off his horse and carried him into the chapel. Rohn, who was in severe pain and weakened by loss of blood, made no demur. The servant carried him up a ladder to the loft, where he wrapped him in his cloak and covered him with bales of straw. Then he gave him his canteen, put two loaded pistols where Rohn could reach them, and covered those, too, with straw. That done, he went off with the horses, but not before he had urged Rohn to lie still, promising to remain close at hand and not to desert him under any circumstances.

Meantime, night had fallen and the firing and shouting had died away. For a while all remained quiet. The lieutenant was just about to put his head out of a skylight and call his servant back, thinking the danger past, when he heard voices and saw lanterns and torches approaching the chapel.

Perceiving at once that the men were guerrillas, he hurriedly concealed himself once more beneath the bales of straw. The holes and chinks in the floor on which he lay enabled him to observe the Spaniards as they carried their wounded into the chapel. One of them climbed the ladder and threw down some bales of straw to his companions while the lieutenant held his breath for fear he should be discovered and butchered on the spot.

But the Spaniard failed to notice him and descended the ladder with his lantern to bandage the wounded. He went from one to another with his instruments, but never before had the lieutenant seen a surgeon ply his trade in such a sullen and surly manner.

"Why are you sitting there like Job the Jew on his dunghill?" he railed at one of the wounded, and poured scorn on another who groaned that he felt he would soon be entering the realms of eternal bliss.

"You fool!" he jeered. "Eternal bliss costs more than you think. Do you really imagine that all you need to get you to heaven is a hole in the belly?"

"What do you have for me in that medicine chest of yours?" cried another man. "Monkey's fat? Bear's grease? Raven's dung?"

"All I have for you is a Paternoster," the surgeon snapped.

"You've too many holes to mend." And, as he busied himself with the next man, he growled, "Yes, Death is a heathen – he never takes a holiday. Wars make hummocky churchyards, that's what I always say."

"How soon will you come to me?" called a wounded man lying in a corner.

"Wait your turn, damn you!" the surgeon cried angrily. "I know you of old – you want a plaster on every little gnat-bite. A pity the bullet didn't fly up the Devil's backside, then I'd not be having to trouble with you now."

The guerrillas had meanwhile kindled a fire outside the chapel. Sentries had been posted on the edge of the woods and an orderly officer was going the rounds. The insurgents, who numbered upwards of a hundred and fifty, lay sprawled around the fire, many of them asleep and some smoking tobacco rolled in paper. They were armed and clothed with what they had taken from the French: infantrymen's gaiters, long cuirassiers' swords, heavy German riding boots. Near the chapel stood a cork oak with an effigy of the Virgin and Child affixed to its trunk, and before this two Spaniards knelt in prayer. A British officer, a captain in the Northumberland Fusiliers, stood leaning on his sword and gazing into the fire. His scarlet cloak and the white panache in his cap made him look, beside the ragged guerrillas, like a gold ducat among copper stivers. (From Rohn's description, this officer could only have been Captain William O'Callaghan, whom General Blake, as we already knew, had sent to instil order and discipline into the guerrilla bands of the district.)

The surgeon, having completed his work in the chapel, came out and limped over to the fire. An exceedingly stout little man, he wore a brown jacket, short trousers, and torn blue hose, but his collar was adorned with colonel's insignia. As soon as the firelight fell upon his face, Lieutenant von Rohn perceived that it was Saracho himself that had bandaged the wounded in the chapel and, spiteful as a monkey, dispensed such poor consolation. On his head he wore a velvet cap embroidered with gold thread. This the lieutenant recognized at once as Marshal Lefebvre's nightcap, which was renowned

14

throughout the army because, when it fell into the insurgents' hands together with some other baggage belonging to Lefebvre, the furious marshal's aides-de-camp and all the other officers in the baggage train had been placed under arrest.

The Tanner's Tub held his hands to the fire to warm them. For a while all was quiet save for the groans of the wounded, a man cursing in his sleep, and the murmured prayers of the two Spaniards on their knees before the Madonna.

At this stage Lieutenant von Rohn's fatigue was so extreme that he would have fallen asleep, despite his thirst and the proximity of his enemies, had he not been suddenly roused by a shout from one of the sentries. He peered through the skylight and caught sight of the Marquis of Bolibar, who was just emerging from the dark wood into the glow of the fire.

Rohn described him as a tall, elderly man whose hair was as white as the moustache beneath his aquiline nose. There was something fierce and awe-inspiring about his features, although, try as he would, Rohn could not define it.

"There he is!" cried the Tanner's Tub, and withdrew his hands from the fire. "The Marquis of Bolibar," he said, turning to the British officer. "Señor Marques, a thousand pardons for having disturbed your night's rest" – here he made a clumsy obeisance – "but I shall doubtless have quit this district by tomorrow, and I have to acquaint you with certain information of great importance. It relates to your family."

The Marquis abruptly turned his head and looked Saracho in the eye. All the blood had left his face, but the firelight suffused his cheeks with a reddish glow. The British captain addressed him in a courteous tone.

"Are you, My Lord Marquis, a kinsman of the Lieutenant-General de Bolibar who commanded the Spanish Second Corps two years ago?"

"The lieutenant-general is my brother," replied the Marquis, without taking his eyes off Saracho.

"An officer of your name saw service in the British Army, too. He captured the French artillery depot at Acre."

"That was my cousin," said the Marquis. He continued to

15

stare at the Tanner's Tub, almost as if he were awaiting a surprise attack from that quarter and had to meet it with a steadfast gaze.

"The family of the Señor Marques has provided many an army with outstanding officers," said Saracho. "One of his nephews served until lately in the French Army."

The Marquis shut his eyes.

"Is he dead?" he asked quietly.

"He had a fine career," the Tanner's Tub replied with a laugh. "He became a French lieutenant despite his seventeen years. I myself have a son and would gladly have made a soldier of him, but he's a hunchback and fit only for a monastery."

"Is he dead?" asked the Marquis. He stood there unmoving, but his shadow leapt wildly about in the fire's fitful light. It was as if the old man's shadow, not the old man himself, were awaiting Saracho's tidings in fear and uncertainty.

"Men of many nations fight with the French Army," Saracho said, shrugging his shoulders. "Germans and Dutchmen, Neapolitans and Poles. Why should a Spaniard not serve with the French for once?"

"Is he dead?" cried the Marquis.

"Dead? Yes!" Saracho blurted out, and he laughed with such fierce and delighted abandon that the grisly sound reverberated among the trees of the forest. "Yes, and now he's racing the Devil to hell!"

"I was there when his mother bore him," the Marquis said in a low, choking voice. "It was I that carried him to his christening, but he was as inconstant from his earliest childhood as a shadow on the wall. God grant him eternal rest."

"May the Devil grant him eternal rest in Hades," cried Saracho with mingled anger and contempt.

"Amen," said the British captain, but it was uncertain whether his amen related to Bolibar's prayer or Saracho's curse.

The Marquis walked over to the shrine and bowed down before the Madonna. The Spaniards who had been praying there rose and made room for him.

"For myself," Saracho remarked to the captain, "I cannot boast of any noble kinsmen. My mother was a maidservant and my father a cobbler, that is why I serve my king and Holy Mother Church. We cannot all be noblemen."

"Lord," prayed the Marquis, kneeling before the image of the Mother of Heaven, "you know that we wretched mortals cannot live without sin."

"And *you* should know, Captain," Saracho said with a scornful, bitter laugh, "that our high-born noblemen – the Duke of Infantado and the Marquis of Villafanca, the two Counts of Orgaz, father and son, and the Duke of Albuquerque – all went to Bayonne to pay homage to Joseph, the new king."

"You cannot have forgotten, O Lord," the Marquis of Bolibar cried to the Madonna, "that one of your own twelve Apostles was a perjurer and a scoundrel!"

"Yes," Saracho pursued, "our proud grandees were the first to go to Bayonne and sell their vows for money, and why not? Are French louis-d'or of baser gold than Spanish doubloons?"

"St Augustine was a heretic, yet you forgave him," the Marquis cried with a fervour born of despair. "Do you hear me, Lord? Paul was a persecutor of the Church, Matthew a miser and a devotee of money, and Peter forswore himself, yet you forgave them one and all. Do you hear me, Lord?"

"But they'll never escape eternal damnation!" Saracho roared triumphantly. "They're doomed, and hell awaits them. Flames, fire and sparks, fire above and below, fire on every side, fire in perpetuity!" And he stared enraptured into the nocturnal gloom as if he could see the flames of hell blazing far away beyond the dark woods.

"Have mercy on him, have mercy, Lord, and let your everlasting light shine upon him!"

Lieutenant von Rohn, listening to this strange prayer in his hiding place, was smitten with surprise and consternation, for the Marquis's tone was far from that of a humble suppliant. He bellowed at the Almighty, sometimes angrily, sometimes threateningly, and sometimes as if striving to bully Him into doing his, Bolibar's, will.

At last the Marquis rose and went over to Saracho with knitted brow, twitching lips, and eyes alight with anger. The Tanner's Tub affected to be surprised to see him still there.

17

"Señor Marques," he said, "the hour grows late, and if you wish to pay your respects to the French commander early in the morning –"

"Enough!" cried the Marquis, and his face looked more fearsome than ever. Saracho broke off at once. The two men stood facing one another, mute and motionless. Only their shadows flitted back and forth in the fire's restless light, crouching and leaping, retreating and lunging, and it seemed to Rohn in the heat of his fever that their hatred and belligerence had silently entered into those darting shadows.

All at once, however, the sentries shouted their challenge once more and a man came running out of the trees toward the fire. As soon as Saracho caught sight of him, he forgot his quarrel with the Marquis of Bolibar.

"*Ave Maria purissima!*" panted the messenger, this being the customary Spanish greeting, and one that can be heard a hundred times a day in street or tavern.

"Amen, she conceived without sin," Saracho replied impatiently. "You came alone? Where's the priest?"

"His Reverence got the colic from a hot blood sausage –"

"A curse on his soul, his body and eyes!" roared Saracho. "That man has less heart than a tripe-cook would sell you for half a quarto. Fear, that's his sickness!"

"He's dead, I can swear to it," said the messenger. "I saw him laid out in his bedchamber."

Saracho ran both hands through his hair and proceeded to curse roundly enough to bring the sky down about his ears. His face turned as red as a stone in a brick-kiln.

"Dead?" he cried, struggling to catch his breath. "Did you hear that, Captain? The priest is dead!"

The British officer stared silently into space. The guerrillas had jumped up and clustered around the fire, shivering under their cloaks.

"What now?" asked the captain.

"I swore on General Cuesta's sword that we would take the town or die. Our plans had been skilfully laid and set in train, and now this priest has to die an untimely death."

"Your plans were worthless," the Marquis of Bolibar said

suddenly. "Your plans would have earned you a bullet in the head, nothing more."

Saracho glared at the Marquis indignantly. "What do you know of our plans?" he demanded. "I didn't shout them from the rooftops."

"Father Ambrosius sent for me when he knew he was going to die," said the Marquis. "He asked me to perform the task with which you entrusted him, but your plans are ill-conceived. I tell you this to your face, Colonel Saracho: you know nothing of the art of war."

"And you do, I suppose, Señor Marques?" Saracho was beside himself with rage. "The enemy will gobble up that town like cold apple sauce."

"You buried a sack of gunpowder beneath the town wall, wedged between sandbags and provided with a fuse. The vicar was to light the fuse under cover of darkness and blow a breach in the wall."

"Quite so," Saracho broke in, "that being the only way of taking the town. La Bisbal would withstand the heaviest of cannon, for the chronicles tell us that it was built more than five thousand years ago by King Hercules and St James."

"Your knowledge of history is admirable, Colonel Saracho, but did it never occur to you that the French would round up all the monks and detain them as soon as they arrived? Tomorrow they'll shut them up, either in their monastery or in a church, post a cannon at the entrance with slow-match burning, and let none of them out. Did you think of that, Colonel Saracho? Even had the priest contrived to escape, you're confronted by the whole of the Nassau Regiment and part of the Hessian. All you have is a handful of ill-trained, indisciplined regulars, each of whom goes his own sweet way."

"True, true," Saracho cried angrily, "but my men are adroit and courageous enough to trample the German colossus underfoot."

"Are you so sure?" demanded the Marquis. "As soon as the charge explodes, the general alarm will sound in every street and the Germans will run to their guns. Two salvoes of grapeshot will put paid to your assault. Hadn't you thought of that, Colonel Saracho?"

The Tanner's Tub, at a loss for a rejoinder, chewed his fingers and said nothing.

"And even should a few of your men succeed in penetrating the town," the Marquis went on, "they'll come under fire from every nook and cranny, every barred window and cellar light, for La Bisbal's inhabitants are more than ever favourably disposed toward the French. Your guerrillas uprooted their vines and set their olive trees ablaze. Why, only lately you had two young men from La Bisbal shot because they refused to join you."

"Yes, that's true," said one of the guerrillas. "The town is against us. The citizens scowl at us, the women turn their backs on us, the dogs bark at us –"

"And the landlords serve us sour wine," grumbled another.

"But for military reasons," said the captain, "the possession of La Bisbal is of the utmost importance to us. If the French hold the town, they can take General Cuesta in the flank and rear whenever his troops make a move."

"Then General Cuesta must send us reinforcements," Saracho exclaimed. "He has the Princesa and Santa Fe Regiments and half the Santiago Cavalry. He must –"

"He'll send us not a single man or cart-horse. He himself is in difficulty, and you know full well that one cripple seldom helps another across the road. What's to be done, Colonel?"

"How can I tell you when I myself have no idea?" Saracho said sullenly, staring at his fingers. The guerrillas around the fire set up a clamour when they saw how perplexed, irresolute and at odds their commanders were. Some cried out that the war was lost and they wanted to go home, others that they had no wish to go home and fetch firewood for their wives, and one man ran to his donkey and proceeded to saddle it as if he meant to set off for his village without delay.

All at once, a voice made itself heard above the hubbub. It belonged to the Marquis of Bolibar.

"If you're willing to obey me, Colonel, I know what to do."

On hearing these words in his lair, Lieutenant von Rohn

once more fell prey to the mysterious sense of dread inspired in him by his very first glimpse of the Marquis's face and eyes. Heedless of the danger that he might be discovered, he thrust his head through the skylight rather than miss a word. His thirst and pain had vanished: his one thought was that fate had ordained him to overhear and foil the schemes of the Marquis of Bolibar.

Such were the clamour and commotion made by the guerrillas, who continued to argue whether it was better to fight on or disband, that Rohn could not at first catch what passed between the Marquis and the other two. After a short while, however, Saracho bade his men be silent, accompanying the order with oaths and imprecations, and the din ceased abruptly.

"Please continue, Your Grace," the captain said, very courteously. Saracho's demeanour, too, had undergone a sudden and complete transformation. He betrayed no lingering trace of scorn, hatred or ill-will as he stood there in a respectful, almost subservient attitude. All three men – the British officer, the rebel commander, and Lieutenant von Rohn – bent an expectant gaze on the Marquis of Bolibar.

THREE SIGNALS

At this point in his narrative Lieutenant von Rohn gave a description of the sinister spectacle presented by this nocturnal conference, which had deeply imprinted itself upon his mind. He recalled how Saracho, squatting down like a goblin, stoked the fire with brushwood – for the night was cold – and looked up at the Marquis intently as he did so; how the British officer, whose impassive face belied his obvious excitement, paid no heed when his scarlet cloak slipped from his shoulders and fell to the ground; how the guerrillas crowded around the fire, in part so as to hear what was said, in part because of the chill night air; and how the cork oak bearing the Madonna, which had been uprooted and half toppled by the wind, seemed to lean toward the Marquis and hang upon his every word. Indeed, the lieutenant fancied in his fearful and feverish state of mind that Christ and the Virgin were in league with the guerrillas and privy to their conspiracy.

Standing in their midst, the Marquis of Bolibar acquainted the others with his murderous plans.

"You will send your men home, Colonel Saracho," he commanded. "You will order them home to their fields and vineyards, their fish ponds and mule stables. Your cannon and powder waggons you will hide in readiness for the time when we are stronger than the Germans."

"And when will that time come?" Saracho inquired doubtfully, shaking his head and blowing on the fire.

"It will come soon enough," the Marquis declared, "for I shall find you an ally. You will receive assistance from a quarter you now dismiss."

Saracho stood up. "If you mean Empecinado and his guerrillas at Campillos," he growled, "that man is my enemy. He will not come when I need him."

"Who spoke of Empecinado? It is the citizens of La Bisbal who will come to your aid. One fine night they will rebel and fall upon the Germans."

"Those bloated, pot-bellied Judases of La Bisbal?" Saracho exclaimed, sinking to the ground again in rage and disappointment. "All they ever think of at night, when they lie alongside their wives, is how best to betray us and our native land."

"I shall persuade them to quit their beds and rise in revolt!" cried the Marquis. He gestured with menace at the town slumbering in the valley far below. "The great insurrection will come, be assured of that. I have my plans ready-made in my head, and I'll stake my body and soul on their success."

For a while the three men gazed silently into the fire, each engrossed in his own thoughts. The guerrillas whispered among themselves and the night wind rustled in the trees, shaking raindrops from branch and twig.

"And what is our part in this venture?" the captain asked at length.

"You will await my signals. I shall give three of them. At the first you will assemble your men, occupy the approaches to the town, place your cannon in position, and blow up both bridges over the Alhar – but not until I give the signal, for it is of prime importance that the Germans should feel secure until then."

"Go on, go on!" Saracho said eagerly.

"On receiving the second signal you will at once proceed to bombard the town with shot, shell, and fire-balls. At the same time, you will take the outer defences."

"And then?"

"By then the revolt will have broken out. While the Germans are busy defending themselves against insurgent townsfolk on every side, I shall give the third signal and you will order a general assault."

"Very good," said Saracho.

"And the signals?" The captain took out his slate.

"Do you know my house in La Bisbal?" the Marquis asked Saracho.

"The house beyond the walls or the one adorned with Saracens' heads in the Calle de los Carmelitas?"

"The latter. You will see a column of thick black smoke ascending from its roof. Smoke from damp, smouldering straw, that will be the first signal."

"Smoke from damp, smouldering straw," the captain repeated.

"One night, when all is quiet in La Bisbal, you will hear the strains of the organ in St Daniel's Convent: that will be the second signal."

"The organ in St Daniel's Convent," wrote the captain. "And the third?"

The Marquis pondered for a moment. Then he said, "Give me your knife, Colonel Saracho."

From under his coat the Tanner's Tub produced a broad-bladed dagger with a hilt of carved ivory – a weapon of the kind the Spaniards call an ox-tongue. The Marquis took it.

"When a messenger brings you this knife, command your men to storm the town – but then and not before. The success of the whole undertaking depends on that, Colonel Saracho."

Lieutenant von Rohn had caught every word from his vantage point beneath the chapel roof. His brow was on fire and the blood pounded in his temples. He now knew the three signals that were designed to bring down destruction upon the garrison of La Bisbal, and he also knew that the success or failure of the undertaking depended on himself, not Saracho.

"There are one or two contingencies to be considered," the British officer said thoughtfully, replacing the slate in his pocket. "For instance, the Germans might deem it advantageous to take a personage such as the Marquis of Bolibar into custody. If they did so, our wait for the signals would doubtless be long and tedious."

"The Germans will never find the Marquis of Bolibar. They may see a blind beggar offering his consecrated *Agnus Dei* candles for sale outside the church door, or a peasant transporting eggs, cheeses and chestnuts to market on donkeyback.

24

Picture me as a sergeant posting sentries outside the powder magazine, or a dragoon leading the regimental commander's charger to the horse-pond."

The captain laughed.

"Yours is not the kind of face one readily forgets, My Lord Marquis. I could recognize you in any disguise, I feel sure."

"Could you indeed?" said the Marquis, and pondered in silence for a while. "Are you acquainted with General Rowland Hill, Captain?"

"I have been privileged to see General the Lord Hill of Hawkstone on many occasions, the last one being at Salamanca four months ago, when I was making some purchases in the neighbourhood of his headquarters." The captain broke off. "Have you lost something, My Lord Marquis?"

The Marquis had bent down. When he straightened up, Lieutenant von Rohn saw that he had draped the captain's scarlet cloak around his shoulders. Rohn failed to perceive any other difference in him until his attention was aroused by the Britisher's look of boundless amazement.

From one moment to the next, the Marquis's face had taken on a wholly strange and unfamiliar appearance. Rohn had never before set eyes on those gaunt, furrowed cheeks, those mobile orbs that darted so restlessly in all directions, that hard, firm mouth, and that massive chin which gave evidence of vigour and grim determination. Then the unfamiliar face opened its mouth and a snarling, drawling voice emerged.

"The next time your assault exposes you to such heavy fire, Captain –"

The Britisher grasped the Marquis roughly by the shoulders and uttered an oath or imprecation whose meaning was lost on Lieutenant von Rohn. "What hell-hound of a playactor taught you that accursed trick?" he cried. "If I didn't happen to know that Lord Hill speaks no word of Spanish . . . Give me back my cloak, it's devilish cold!"

The guerrillas laughed at his annoyance and astonishment, but one of them crossed himself and said, with a timid glance at the Marquis, "Our gracious lord the Señor Marques can do other things as well. Give him two measures of blood, twelve

25

pounds of flesh and a sack of bones, and he'll make you a man
– Christian or Moor, it's all the same to him."

"Well, Captain," said the Marquis, who had reverted to his
previous appearance, "do you still believe the Germans will
arrest me if I decide to disappear? I shall pass through the Puerta
del Sol at vespers this very day, and not a soul will prevent me
from doing so."

"I wish you would tell me your chosen disguise," the captain
said anxiously. "Should my men fail to recognize you while
storming La Bisbal, I fear they may do you harm."

"My one desire," exclaimed the Marquis, "is to be buried
unrecognized. In losing my life, I shall also lose a name that
has for ever been stained with dishonour."

The fire in their midst had dwindled and begun to go out.
The wind blew cold and damp, and a pale dawn was rising
beyond the gloomy woods. The captain stared into the dying
embers.

"The glory your exploit will bring you –" he ventured.

"Glory?" the Marquis broke in angrily. "Know this, Captain: no glory derives from battle and conquest. I despise war,
which for ever compels us to do evil. The humble peasant who
innocently tills his field is more glorious than any general or
marshal, for his poor hands tend soil which the rest of us have
profaned and defiled with our blood-letting."

At these words, all who stood round the dying fire fell silent
and stared with surprise and respect at the man who despised
war, yet took it upon himself to perform war's bloody work
in expiation of the treason committed by someone of his name.

"I am a soldier," Saracho said at long last, "and I shall
persuade you of the glory that war can bring a gallant soldier
when our venture is successfully concluded, Señor Marques,
for I shall recognize you."

"If you recognize me, have pity and refrain from addressing
me by my name, which is disgraced to all eternity. Look away
and let me walk on unrecognized. And now, farewell."

"Farewell," the captain called after him, "and may heaven
assist you in your undertaking."

While the Marquis was striding off, Saracho turned to the

captain and said in a low voice, "I doubt if the Marques de Bolibar –"

He broke off, for the Marquis had halted and looked back.

"You turn your head on hearing your name, Señor Marques," Saracho called, laughing loudly. "That is how I shall know you again."

"You're right, and I thank you. I must teach my ear to be deaf to the sound of my name."

That, it seems, was the moment when the Marquis of Bolibar hit upon the idea whose execution I observed in his garden the following day, not that I grasped the purpose of such a strange proceeding. Lieutenant von Rohn, meanwhile, was consumed with fear and impatience. Knowing that he alone could preserve the Nassau Regiment from the danger that threatened it at La Bisbal, he could hardly wait for his servant to release him from his hiding place and convey him there. He was tormented by the fear that Bolibar, having reached the town before him and vanished unhindered into the crowd, would put his terrible scheme into effect.

But now at last Saracho gave the order to depart. The guerrillas promptly sprang to their feet and began bustling to and fro. Some fetched the wounded from the chapel, others loaded the mules with baskets of victuals, wineskins, and valises. Some sang as they worked, a few bickered, the mules set up a piercing din, the muleteers cursed. In the midst of this turmoil the British captain suspended his camp kettle over the fire and prepared some tea for breakfast. Saracho, who had attached a lantern and a mirror to the tree beside the Virgin and Child, was shaving in haste. Glancing at the mirror and the Madonna in turn, he scraped away at his beard and prayed as he did so.

SNOW ON THE ROOFS

At the hour of the rosary, or vespers, on the evening of the same day, the Marquis of Bolibar made his way without let or hindrance through the Puerta del Sol. No one recognized him, and he might well have escaped detection, like an eel in a turbid stream, amid the water-carriers and fishmongers, spice and oil merchants, wool-dressers and friars who crowded around the church door to say their Hail Marys and greet familiar faces. It was, however, his misfortune to become privy to the secret that bound the five of us together – the other four and myself – with bonds of memory. What secret? Ours and that of the dead Françoise-Marie, which at other times we kept locked away in the depths of our hearts, and of which we that night bragged to one another, fuddled with Alicante wine and stricken with homesickness by the sight of the snow on the roofs.

And the ragged muleteer who sat in the corner of my room, a rosary in his hands, overheard that secret and had to die.

We ordered him shot beside the town wall, secretly and in haste, without trial or absolution. None of us dreamed that it was the Marquis of Bolibar who fell bleeding into the snow beneath our bullets, nor did we guess what a curse he had laid upon us before he died.

I had command of the gate guard that evening. Toward six o'clock I detailed the night pickets that were to patrol the town wall at intervals of half an hour. My sentries, with their loaded carbines hidden beneath their cloaks, stood silent and motionless like saints in their niches.

It began to snow. Snowy weather was no great rarity in that mountainous region, it seemed, but we had never seen snowflakes in Spain before that evening.

I had two copper pans filled with glowing ashes brought to my room, there being no stoves in the houses of La Bisbal. The smoke stung my eyes and the snowstorm made the windows rattle with a faint, menacing sound, but the room was warm and snug. In the corner lay my couch of freshly gathered heather with a cloak draped over it. The makeshift table and benches were fashioned from planks and barrels, and on the table were gourds filled with wine, for I was awaiting a visit from my comrades, who proposed to spend Christmas Eve with me.

I could hear the voices of my dragoons as they lay talking on the floor of the loft overhead, wrapped in their cloaks. Without a sound, I tiptoed up the wooden stairs.

I often prowled among my men in the dark and listened to them conversing, for I was in constant dread lest our secret had been discovered, and lest the dragoons, when they thought themselves alone and out of earshot at night, should whisper to each other of the dead Françoise-Marie and her surreptitious goings-on.

Although the loft was as dark as a bake-oven, I recognized Sergeant Brendel's voice.

"Did you find the fellow who made off with your purse?" he was asking.

"I gave chase," replied a glum voice, "but I couldn't catch him. He's gone, and he'll take good care not to come back."

"All these Spaniards are the same!" another man said angrily. "They pray their mouths off from dawn till dusk, empty the fonts of holy water out of sheer piety and devotion, and all the while the rogues and bloodsuckers are debating how best to cheat and rob us."

"When we were quartered in Corbosa five days ago," I heard Corporal Thiele say, "one such unhung thief – one of the waggoners, he was – made off with a chest belonging to our colonel. It contained the bonnets and petticoats of his late lamented wife, and now the thief has borne them off to his stinking lair!"

Our colonel was so reluctant to be parted from the dead Françoise-Marie's clothes that he carried them in his baggage wherever he went. Now, on hearing the dragoons speak of his wife, I felt my heart begin to pound in the certainty that our secret had been discovered. But I heard not another word about Françoise-Marie. The dragoons proceeded to grumble at the campaign and their generals, and Sergeant Brendel fiercely castigated Marshal Soult and his staff.

"Let me tell you something," he exclaimed. "Those gentlemen who go to war in their carriages and carioles are often more frightened under fire than the likes of us. At Talavera I saw them cower like mules when the case-shot was flying."

"We have worse foes than shells," said someone else. "Our worst foes are these nonsensical marches back and forth, eight hours at a stretch, to hang some wretched peasant or priest. Shells do us less harm than damp ground, lice, and half rations."

"And the mutton, don't forget the mutton," said Dragoon Stüber. "It stinks to high heaven. Why, sparrows fall lifeless from the air when they fly over it!"

"Soult cares nothing for his men, that's the truth of the matter," Corporal Thiele said gloomily. "He's a niggard – wealth and honours are all he craves. He may be a marshal and Duke of Dalmatia, but believe me, he isn't fit to fill a corporal's boots."

Not another word about Françoise-Marie. I listened in vain, hearing naught save the eternal criticisms of the Spanish campaign with which the soldiers customarily whiled away the time before falling asleep in their billets, fatigued by marching and fighting. I let them argue and politicize to their hearts' content. They performed their duties none the worse for that.

At length, hearing Lieutenant Günther's voice below, I hurried downstairs to my room and lit a lamp.

Günther was patting the snow from his uniform. Lieutenant Donop, with Virgil peeping out of his pocket as usual, had also turned up. Donop was the most intelligent and erudite of my comrades. He knew Latin, was well-versed in ancient history, and always travelled with a few fine editions of the Roman classics in his baggage.

We sat down, drank wine, and fell to cursing our Spanish landlords and our wretched billets. Donop complained that his room had neither stove nor fireplace and a piece of oiled paper in lieu of a windowpane. "Let someone else try reading the *Aeneid* in there!" he said with a sigh.

"Every wall is covered with pictures of saints, but there isn't a clean bed in the house," Günther said peevishly of his own quarters. "Prayer books lie heaped in the kitchen, but I've yet to see a ham or a sausage."

"It's impossible to carry on a sensible conversation with my landlord," Donop said. "He spends the whole day mumbling the name of the Holy Virgin, and whenever I come home he's on his knees before some St James or Dominic."

"For all that," I interposed, "they say the citizens of La Bisbal are well-disposed toward the French. Your health, comrade! I drink to you."

"And I to you, comrade, but they also say that disguised priests and insurgents are hiding in the town."

"Very meek insurgents," said Günther. "They neither shoot at us nor murder us – they confine themselves to despising us."

"I'll wager my landlord is a priest in disguise," said Donop, chuckling to himself. "I know of no other trade that makes a man so fat."

He passed his glass across the table and I refilled it. Just then the door burst open and Captain Brockendorf came blundering into the room in a cloud of wind-blown snowflakes.

He must already have been drinking somewhere, because his full moon of a face, with its huge, crimson scar, was gleaming like a freshly hammered copper kettle. His cap sat askew over his left ear, his black moustache was waxed, and his two thick black braids hung stiffly from temples to chest. "Well, Jochberg," he bellowed, "have you caught him?"

"Not yet," I replied, knowing that he meant the Marquis of Bolibar.

"My Lord Marquis is taking his time. The weather isn't clement enough for him – he's afraid it may spoil his shoes."

Brockendorf bent over the table and put his nose to the gourds.

"What holy water is that in Bacchus's font?"

"Alicante wine from the priest's cellar."

"Alicante, eh?" Brockendorf cried gaily. "*Allons*, that's worth making a beast of oneself for!"

When Brockendorf "made a beast" of himself in honour of good wine, he stripped off his tunic, waistcoat and shirt and sat there naked save for his breeches and boots and the mat of shaggy black hair on his chest. Two old women who were passing our windows in the street stopped short and stared into the room aghast. They crossed themselves, doubtless wondering what had met their eyes, a human being or some outlandish monster.

We all proceeded to do justice to the wine, and for a while no conversation could be heard beyond "I toast you, comrade!" or "I thank you, brother!" or "Your health, comrade. *Proficiat!*"

"I wish I were at home in Germany and had some Barbara or Dorothea in my bed tonight," Günther said suddenly in a maudlin voice, disheartened by his lack of success with the Spanish women whom he had been pursuing all day long. Brockendorf chaffed him. He himself, he said, would rather be a crane or a stork so that the wine took longer to travel down his throat. By now the Alicante was beginning to go to our heads. Donop was loudly declaiming Horace above the din when Eglofstein, the regimental adjutant, strode into the room.

I sprang up and submitted my report.

"No other news, Jochberg?" he asked.

"None."

"Has no one passed the guards at the gate?"

"A Benedictine prior come from Barcelona to visit his sister in the town – the alcalde vouches for him – and an apothecary and his wife and daughter passing through here on the way to Bilbao. Their papers were issued by General d'Hilliers' headquarters and are perfectly in order."

"No one else?"

"Two townsmen left here this morning to do a day's work in their vineyards. They were given laissez-passers and presented them on their return."

"Very good. Thank you."

"Eglofstein, I drink to you!" called Brockendorf, brandishing his glass. "Your health! Come, my old crane, sit here by me."

Eglofstein looked at our tipsy comrade and smiled. Donop, still steady on his feet, came over to him with two glasses of wine.

"Captain," he said, "we're gathered here tonight to await the Marquis of Bolibar. Bide with us and greet him, when he appears, on behalf of the officers of the regiment."

"To hell with all counts and marquises – liberty for ever!" roared Brockendorf. "Devil take the perfumed puppets with their bag-wigs and *chapeaux bas*!"

"I have to visit the pickets and the men detailed to guard the flour mills and bakehouses, but no matter, they can wait," said Eglofstein, and joined us at the table.

"Sit by me, Eglofstein!" Brockendorf bellowed drunkenly. "You've grown proud – you've forgotten how the two of us picked grains of corn out of horse dung to keep from starving in Prussia." Wine had made the big, strong man lachrymose and melancholy. He propped his forehead on his fists and began to sob. "Do you never think of that any more? Ah, what a worm-eaten thing is friendship!"

"The war isn't done yet, comrade," said Eglofstein. "We may yet make another midday meal of nettles and leaves stewed in salt water, as we did at Küstrin."

"And when the war's over," said Donop, "the Emperor will be quick to start another."

"All the better!" cried Brockendorf, who had suddenly regained his high spirits. "My purse is empty, comrade, and I still have to win myself the Légion d'Honneur."

He proceeded to recite the engagements in which he had taken part during the Spanish campaign – Zorzola, Almaraz, Talavera, Mesa de Ibor – but got stuck halfway through, even though he enlisted his fingers as an aid to enumeration and had to begin all over again. The heat in the cramped little room had become unbearable. Donop opened the window, and the chill night air streamed in and cooled our brows.

33

"There's snow on the roofs," Donop said softly, and our hearts ached and melted at the words, for they conjured up memories of winters gone by – German winters. We rose and went to the window and gazed at the benighted streets through a dense veil of dancing snowflakes. Brockendorf alone remained seated, still counting on his fingers.

"Brockendorf!" Eglofstein called over his shoulder. "How many homeward miles from here to Dietkirchen?"

"That I couldn't tell you." Brockendorf gave up counting. "Arithmetic never was my strong suit. I learned my algebra from innkeepers and potboys."

He got up and tottered over to the window. The snow had wrought a strange transformation in the Spanish town. All at once, the people in the streets had taken on a familiar and well-remembered appearance. A peasant was trudging through the snow to the church with a little waxen ox in his hand. Two old crones stood squabbling in a doorway. A milkmaid came out of a byre with a lantern in one hand and a pail in the other.

"It was a night like this," Donop said suddenly. "The snow lay ankle-deep in the streets. A year ago, it was. I had been sick that day and was lying in bed, reading Virgil's *Georgics*, when I heard a light footfall on the stairs. Then came a gentle knock on the door of my bedchamber. 'Who's there?' I called, and again, 'Who's there?' – 'It is I, dear friend!' And then she came in. Ah, comrades, her hair was as red as beech leaves in autumn. 'Are you sick, my poor friend?' she asked with tender concern. 'Yes,' I cried, 'I'm sick, and you alone, my beautiful angel, can cure me.' And I sprang out of bed and kissed her hands."

"And then?" Lieutenant Günther demanded hoarsely.

"Ah, then . . ." whispered Donop, far away in spirit. "There was snow on the roofs. The night was as cold as her flesh and blood were warm."

Günther said not a word. He strode up and down the room, glaring at Donop and the rest of us with hatred in his eyes.

"Long live the colonel!" cried Brockendorf. "He had the best wine and the fairest wife in all Germany."

"The first time we were alone together in my room . . ."

Eglofstein began. "Why should I recall it today of all days? Perhaps because a man could barely keep his eyes open in the street, the snow was driving so hard. I was seated at the piano while she stood beside me. Her bosom rose and fell as I played, ever more rapidly, and I heard her sigh. 'Can I trust you, Baron?' she asked, and took my hand. 'Feel how my heart is beating!' she said softly, and guided my hand beneath her shawl to where nature had imprinted that blue buttercup on her skin."

"Pass the wine!" Günther cried, almost choking with anger. Ah, we had all in our time kissed that birthmark, that little blue ranunculus, but Günther, who had been the first to do so, was still racked with jealousy. He hated Eglofstein, he hated Brockendorf – he hated us all for having enjoyed the lovely Françoise-Marie's favours in succession to himself.

"Pass the wine!" he cried again, hoarse with rage, and snatched up the gourd.

"The wine is finished, Mass is done, and we can sing the *Kyrie eleison*," Donop said mournfully, thinking not of the wine but of bygone days and of Françoise-Marie.

"You buffoons!" cried Brockendorf, so drunk that he swept his glass from the table to the floor and smashed it. "What are you drivelling about? Which of you knew her as I did, you runts and weaklings? What do you know of her *soupers d'amour*? Such dishes she served!" He guffawed loudly, and Günther turned pale as death. "Four courses, there were. '*À la Crécour*' was the first. Then came *à l'Aretino*, *à la Dubarry* and, to end with, *à la Cythère* –"

"And *à la* whipping!" Günther hissed, beside himself with jealousy and rage. He raised his glass as if to hurl it in Brocken-dorf's face, but at that moment we heard a loud commotion and voices in the street.

"Who goes there?" called a sentry.

"France!" came the reply.

"Halt, who goes there?" called a second sentry.

"*Vive l'Empereur!*" said a curt, gruff voice.

Günther put his glass down and listened.

"Go and see what's up," Donop told me.

35

Then the door burst open and one of my men came in, thick with snow.

"Lieutenant, a strange officer wishes to speak with the commander of the guard."

We jumped up, exchanging glances of surprise and perplexity. Brockendorf hastily thrust his arms into the sleeves of his tunic.

All of a sudden Eglofstein burst out laughing.

"Had you forgotten, comrades?" he cried. "It's our privilege tonight to welcome His Lordship the Marquis of Bolibar!"

CAPTAIN DE SALIGNAC

Captain of Cavalry Baptiste de Salignac may well have thought us blind drunk or utterly insane when he entered the room, which rang with merriment. Boisterous laughter greeted him. Brockendorf was brandishing his empty wine glass, Donop had flopped back in his chair and was roaring with mirth, and Eglofstein, with a sarcastic air, performed a low and deferential bow.

"My respects, Lord Marquis. We've been expecting you this past hour."

Salignac stood in the doorway, looking uncertainly from one to another. His blue tunic with the white revers and his stock of two colours were torn, crumpled, and stained with red and yellow mud, his cloak was wrapped around his hips, and his white breeches were sodden with snow and bespattered to the knees with the mire of the highway. The bandage that encircled his head, turban fashion, lent him a resemblance to one of General Rapp's Mamelukes. He was holding a bullet-riddled helmet in his hand, and in the doorway behind him, laden with a pinewood torch and two valises, stood a Spanish *arriero* or muleteer.

"Come in, Your Lordship," called Donop, still laughing. "We're eager to make your acquaintance." Brockendorf, who had jumped to his feet, planted himself in front of the newcomer and looked him curiously up and down.

"Good evening, Excellency. Your servant, My Lord Marquis."

Then, because it seemed to occur to him that it was improper to joke with a traitor and a spy, he proceeded to stroke his black, waxed moustache and bellow at the man with a ferocious expression.

"Your side-arm, if you please! At once!"

Salignac, looking astonished, retreated a step. The light of the torch fell full on his weather-worn face, and I saw that it was bloodless, almost yellow, as if stricken with the ghastly pallor of some dire disease. He turned indignantly to his servant, who was bending down to extinguish the flames of the torch in melted snow.

"The wine in these parts must be dangerous," he said in a testy voice. "Anyone who drinks it loses his wits, by all appearances."

"Yes indeed, Señor Militar," the muleteer replied obsequiously. "I know it too well."

Salignac must have judged Donop to be the least drunk among us, for he strode up to him.

"Captain de Salignac of the Horse Guards," he said curtly. "I am under orders from Marshal Soult to report to your regimental commander. May I know your name, sir?"

"Lieutenant Donop, by your kind and gracious leave, most noble Lord Marquis," was Donop's mocking response. "Entirely at your service, Excellency."

"Enough of this tomfoolery!" Salignac's hands were trembling with suppressed fury, but his voice was cold and his face as bloodless as ever. "Which do you prefer, swords or pistols? I have both to hand."

Donop was about to make some bantering retort, but Brockendorf forestalled him.

"My compliments, Your Lordship!" he bellowed drunkenly, leaning across the table. "How fares Your Lordship's precious state of health?"

The captain's chill composure deserted him from one moment to the next. He drew his sabre and proceeded to belabour Brockendorf furiously with the flat of the blade.

"Gently, gently!" cried Brockendorf. Surprised·and bewildered, he sought refuge behind the table and strove to parry the blows with an empty gourd.

"Stop!" shouted Eglofstein, seizing the furious captain's arm.

"Let me be!" Salignac cried, and continued to thrash Brockendorf with his sabre.

"You can duel all you please, but afterwards. Listen to me first!"

"No, let him be!" Brockendorf yelled from behind his table. "I've broken wild horses enough before now, and never got bitten yet. Oh, damnation!"

The flat of the sabre had caught him across the back of the hand. He promptly dropped the gourd and stared with sullen resentment at his hairy fingers.

Salignac lowered the sabre, threw back his head, and eyed the rest of us with a mixture of triumph and defiance.

"Did I hear aright?" cried Eglofstein. "Salignac, you said. If you are Captain Baptiste de Salignac of the Horse Guards, I must know you. I am Captain Eglofstein of the Nassau Regiment. We met some years ago, when riding courier."

"Quite so," said Salignac, "between Küstrin and Stralsund. I recognized you as soon as I entered the room, Baron, but your behaviour –"

"Comrade!" Eglofstein exclaimed, aghast. "I cannot believe it!" He went right up to Salignac and looked closely at his sallow face. "You've undergone a curious transformation since those days at Küstrin."

 Captain de Salignac pursed his lips in annoyance. "I caught a recurrent fever years ago. I've suffered from bouts of this kind ever since."

"You caught it in the colonies?" Eglofstein inquired.

"No, in Syria, and a long while ago," said Salignac, looking singularly old and weary all of a sudden. "But enough of that. It's a mischance I regard as proper to my profession."

"You've been the victim of another mischance, comrade. We were awaiting the arrival of the Marquis of Bolibar, a dangerous Spanish conspirator. It's reported that he intends to pass through our lines in French uniform."

"And you mistook me for this Spanish conspirator?" The captain rummaged in the pockets of his blue coat and produced his credentials. "As you see, I'm instructed to join your regiment and take command of a squadron of dragoons whose

39

captain, so I was told, has been either wounded or captured by the British."

I myself had commanded the dragoons since the wounding of Captain Hulot d'Hozery, their squadron commander, so I went up to Salignac and stated my name and rank.

We were standing in a semicircle round the new squadron commander. Brockendorf was rubbing his smarting hand behind his back. Günther, the only one to remain aloof, was standing beside the window, his angry gaze directed at the darkened street. He was still brooding on Françoise-Marie and on what Brockendorf had drunkenly divulged about her *soupers d'amour* and their four "courses" of carnal delight.

"It seems I came at the right moment," said Salignac, shaking hands with each of us in turn. "I should tell you," he pursued, and the eyes in his sallow face shone with eagerness at the thought of an adventure in store, "– I should tell you that I have some experience in the detection of spies. It was I that captured the two Austrian officers who infiltrated our ranks at Wagram. Duroc himself entrusted me with several such missions."

Although I did not know who Duroc was, the name sounded familiar. I supposed him to be one of the Emperor's confidants – possibly the man responsible for his personal safety.

My new squadron commander went on to ask Eglofstein for all the information we had about the Marquis of Bolibar and his plans. His eyes gleamed and his gaunt face grew taut. "The Emperor will be pleased with his old *grognard*!" he said when Eglofstein had concluded his report. Then, turning to me, he inquired the way to the colonel's quarters and requested a dragoon for an escort.

"So there's work for me again," he said, filled with impatience. The dragoon and the Spanish muleteer kneeled down beside him and began to brush the grime from his gaiters. "My last mission was to escort a convoy of forty waggons laden with shot and shell from Fort St Fernando to Fergosa. A tedious business. Much shouting, bickering and ill temper, continual inspections, endless delays on the road." He broke off. "Are you done, you two?"

"And the journey here?" asked Eglofstein.

"I rode the entire way with sabre drawn and carbine cocked. Beyond the bridge near Tornella I was attacked by bandits. They shot my horse and my servant, but I repaid them in kind."

"You're wounded?"

Salignac ran a hand over his turban. "A graze on the forehead, nothing more. The only soul I encountered on the highroad since morning was this fellow here, who carried my baggage." He turned to the *arriero*. "Are you done? Very well, remain here with my valises until I return."

"Your Honour," the Spaniard began, but Salignac cut him short.

"Didn't you hear me? You'll remain here till I send you home. You may dig your herb garden tomorrow."

"Sit down and drink with us, Excellency," Brockendorf urged. "There must be more wine." He was so fuddled that he continued to mistake Salignac for the Marquis of Bolibar and address him as Excellency. Seeing the rest of us converse with him amicably, however, he had quite forgiven him the blow on the hand and his treacherous schemes.

"There's no wine left," said Donop.

"I should have three bottles of port wine in my valise. I take it with the juice of an orange and a little hot tea as an antidote to my fever whenever it recurs." Salignac fetched the bottles from his baggage, and we were soon seated over brimming glasses once more. He himself drew his cloak around his shoulders and sheathed his sabre.

"This marquis will rue the day his path crossed mine," he growled as he opened the door. "Before another hour is up, I shall either march him in here for a glass of port, or –"

His concluding words were drowned by the snow-laden wind that came whistling through the open door, so I never heard what Salignac vowed to do if the Marquis of Bolibar evaded capture.

THE COMING OF GOD

Eglofstein, Donop and I got out the cards as soon as Salignac had left the room. Fortune being kinder to me than usual that night, I won at Eglofstein's expense. He drew fours and doubled several times, as I recall, yet he continued to lose. Donop was just dealing another hand when the sound of a quarrel came to our ears. Lieutenant Günther had again fallen out with Captain Brockendorf.

Brockendorf, leaning back in his chair with his port wine in front of him, was bellowing for a bottle "of the best" as if he were in a tavern. Günther stood over the table, glaring down at him with baleful, narrowed eyes.

"You insist on the respect due to your rank," he hissed angrily, "yet you guzzle like a Moor and swill like an ox!"

"*Vivat amicitia*, comrade," Brockendorf replied in a drowsy voice and raised his glass, for all he wanted to go on drinking his wine in peace.

"You swill like an ox and wear linen fit for a waggoner," Günther said, louder still, "yet you claim to be an officer. From what Jew, buffoon or chimney-sweep did you buy that shirt of yours?"

"Either be silent or speak French," warned Eglofstein, who had sent for two dragoons to sweep the floor clean of melted snow.

"Shall I anoint my hair with *eau de lavande* into the bargain, M'sieur Popinjay?" sneered Brockendorf. "Shall I attend balls and routs and slaver over women's paws as you do?"

"You?" said Donop, turning on him. "You prefer to sit all day in village inns and have the peasants ply you with ale."

"And he claims to be an officer!" Günther chimed in.

"Not so loud!" said Eglofstein. He glanced uneasily at the dragoons who were sweeping the room. "Do you want your squabbles bandied about and brought to the colonel's ears?"

"They understand no French," Günther replied, and turned again to Brockendorf. "What of that fracas at the 'Hairy Jew' in Darmstadt? Didn't you duel there with fist and cudgel, like any guttersnipe? You're a disgrace to the regiment!"

"For all that, my lad," said Brockendorf, hugely pleased with himself, "like it or not, I enjoyed myself in the arms of your beloved. Scowl as much as you please, it makes no odds: I was lying beside her on Candlemas Eve while you stood below in the snow, tossing pebbles at her window."

"You've lain with tavern trollops and street-walkers," Günther bellowed in a fury, "but never with her!"

"Candlemas Eve?" Captain Eglofstein exclaimed, knitting his brow. "Damn you, Brockendorf! I think it was I that stood beneath her window that night, not Günther."

But Brockendorf was too far gone to heed him.

"Yes," he said, "you threw pebbles at her window, we heard you. And I climbed back into her bed and said, 'Hark, that's Günther below.' And she rested her head on her hands and laughed. 'The poor boy,' she said, still laughing, 'he's so clumsy, he never knows where to put his arms and legs when he's with me.'"

Brockendorf's voice was as raucous as a waggon wheel creaking across a bridge, but our anger waned as we listened. We looked at him, and all we heard issuing from his drunken lips was the distant sound of Françoise-Marie's merry laughter.

"I thought the colonel was at home when I saw the shadow on the windowpane," said Eglofstein, hanging his head. "Had I known it was you, Brockendorf, I would have gone upstairs and thrown you out of the window into the snow, hanged if I wouldn't. Still, that's water under the bridge, and love passes like a fever."

Brockendorf, however, was not yet done with Günther.

"Many's the time she laughed," he bellowed. "Many's the time she said, 'He wants me to go up to his room with him, the silly boy, and do you know where he lodges? Behind some farmyard. Over a chicken-coop and below a pigeon-loft – that's the love-nest he has in mind for me!'"

Although the mocking words he hurled at us were Françoise-Marie's, none of us felt angry. We stood there listening, and it was as if our dead beloved were speaking to us once more through the lips of a drunken sot.

Donop always waxed melancholy and philosophical in his cups. "Comrades," he said quietly, "it fills me with remorse that we stole the colonel's wife."

Brockendorf guffawed. "I know, comrade, I know. You wrote her Ciceronian love letters aplenty – I had to translate them for her while we lay in bed together."

"Hush, not so loud!" Donop said fearfully. "If the colonel gets to hear, we'll all be done for."

"So you're afflicted with *stridor dentium*, are you, comrade?" roared Brockendorf. "A fell disease, that – it causes a man to wet his breeches. Myself, I don't give a fig for all the colonels and generals in the world."

"I regret what I did," Donop said sadly. "Here we sit, the five of us, with nothing left to us of that time save disgust, jealousy and hatred."

He put his head in his hands, and the wine in him proceeded to philosophize.

"Right and wrong, comrades, are an ill-matched team. Each has a different gait, but there are times when I seem to discern the hand that holds them both on the rein and ploughs the world's tilth. What name should I give it, the mysterious force that has made us all so wretched and foolish? Should I call it fate, or chance, or the everlasting law of the stars?"

"We Spaniards call it God," said an unfamiliar voice from the corner of the room.

Startled, we looked round. The two dragoons had gone – their brooms stood propped against the wall – but the Spanish muleteer who had brought Captain Salignac's baggage was squatting in the corner, wrapped in a brown, homespun cloak and saying his rosary. The torchlight fell on his broad, red, exceedingly ugly face, and his thick lips were shaping an endless

44

prayer. He had spread a coarse woollen cloth on the floor, and on it lay some bread and garlic.

We were more surprised than dismayed, I think, when first we perceived that it was the Spaniard whose simple words had intruded on our conversation, but we quickly grasped what had happened.

The man had overheard our secret. It had taken only minutes to betray the thing that each of us had so carefully concealed for a twelvemonth: that Françoise-Marie, our colonel's wife, had been the mistress of us all. We were at a stranger's mercy. I seemed to see the colonel's bearded face close to mine, convulsed with murderous rage. My knees trembled and an icy torrent coursed down my spine. This was the moment we had been dreading for a full year: the hour of doom had struck.

We stood there in silence, appalled and nonplussed. One long minute limped by. Befuddled no longer, I was suddenly as sober as if no drop of wine had ever touched my lips, but my head ached and my heart was heavy with fear. I could hear a dog howling outside in the yard. The muffled, plaintive sound seemed to issue from my own throat, almost as if I myself, wild with terror, were moaning and lamenting in the snow.

Eglofstein recovered his composure at last. He squared his shoulders and walked over to the Spaniard with a menacing air, riding crop in hand. "What, not gone yet? Why are you sitting there eavesdropping?"

"I am waiting as instructed, Señor Militar."

"You speak French?"

"A few words only, señor," the Spaniard mumbled, looking frightened and confused. "My wife came to these parts from the town of Bayonne – I learned them from her. *Sacré chien*, she taught me, and *sacré matin* and *gaillard*, *petit gaillard*, and *bon garçon*, and *vive la nation*. That's all I know."

"Enough of your litany!" Günther shouted. "You're a spy. You stole in here to glean what intelligence you could."

"I'm no spy!" the muleteer protested. "Holy Mother of God, I did no more than show that strange officer the way and carry his baggage. Ask Brother Francisco of the Barnabite Fraternity

45

about me – ask the reverend chaplain of the Eremita de Nuestra Señora. They both know old Perico – ask them, Señor Militar!"

"To hell with your priests and your poetry!" cried Brockendorf. "Speak when you're spoken to, spy. Till then, hold your tongue!"

The Spaniard fell silent. He spat a morsel of bread and garlic on the floor and looked uneasily from one to another, but all he saw were grim and merciless faces devoid of compassion.

We put our heads together over the table and held a whispered council of war. The howling of the dog grew louder. It was now quite close at hand.

"He must go," said Donop. "He must quit this town at once. If he blabs we're lost – all of us."

"Impossible," I said. "The sentries are under orders to let no one past the gate."

"I'll never rest while that fellow's at liberty to tell what he overheard here," Donop whispered.

"He must die," Günther said softly. "Protest and lament as he may, he must die, or by tomorrow our every word will be common knowledge throughout the regiment."

"He must," said Brockendorf, "or this business will ruin us."

"We have no grounds for a court martial," I said. "The man's no spy. All he did was carry Salignac's baggage."

"What are we to do?" Donop groaned. "I see disaster looming, comrades. What are we to do?"

"I don't know," said Eglofstein. He shrugged his shoulders. "I only know we're lost, comrades, one and all."

While we were standing there, utterly perplexed, the door sprang open and Sergeant Urban of the Nassau Grenadiers came bustling in. He was holding a big black dog by the collar.

"Captain!" he panted, for it was all he could do to restrain the beast, which was struggling like a mad thing. "Captain, this dog was roaming around outside and wouldn't be driven away. It scratched at the door and wanted to be let in."

No sooner had he caught sight of the muleteer than he let go the collar, put his hands on his hips, and burst out laughing.

"If it isn't Perico!" he exclaimed, almost doubled up with

mirth. "Back so soon, Perico? That was no lengthy pilgrimage of yours!"

The dog had reached the muleteer in a single bound. It jumped up at him again and again, barking, whining, and manifesting every sign of pleasure.

"What about this man, Sergeant?" asked Eglofstein. "Do you know him?"

"Indeed he does, señor," the Spaniard cried joyfully. "You heard him call me Perico: Perico, that's me. God and the Holy Virgin be praised! I'm no spy, you can see that for yourself." The dog pressed against him, whimpering and licking his hands, but he thrust it away and shooed it into a corner.

"You're no spy, true, but you're a thief!" exclaimed the sergeant. "Give that money back, you vile, dirty, ragged scoundrel! If the Emperor raised a regiment of rogues, you'd be its colour-bearer!"

The Spaniard blenched and stared at him in alarm.

"Captain," the sergeant reported, "this fellow is one of the waggoners we took into our employ. This morning, while we were resting outside the inn near the town gate, he stole a purse containing twelve thalers from Dragoon Kümmel of Sergeant Brendel's troop. We gave chase, but we failed to catch him. Now he has returned of his own accord."

The muleteer paled and began to tremble all over.

"You scum!" yelled the sergeant. "Give that money back. You've no further need of it in any case – you'll be hanged or gaoled for life!"

Eglofstein stood up, a wild and exultant gleam in his eye. His heart was heavy no longer, now that this Spanish eavesdropper had been caught stealing and was doomed to die. He exchanged a meaningful glance with Günther and Donop.

"Were you not paid your wage every day?" he asked the Spaniard sternly. "Had you any reason to steal?"

"I stole nothing," the man stammered, beside himself with terror. "I know nothing of any wage – I never was a waggoner in your service."

"Lies by the cartload!" the sergeant said angrily. "You say you never drove a waggon for the regiment?" He ran to the

47

stairs and shouted up them at the loft above. "Kümmel! Are you still awake, Kümmel? Come down here at the double – your thalers have trotted home again."

Dragoon Kümmel came stumbling down the stairs a moment later, torpid and unkempt as a carter's nag, with a horse blanket draped around his shoulders in lieu of a cloak. He brightened at once when he saw the muleteer.

"So you're back!" he cried. "You shit-bucket! You pig-swill! You devil's privy! Who caught you? Where's my money?"

"What do you want with me?" the muleteer groaned, more terrified than ever. "I don't know you – I never saw you before in my life, I swear it by the blood of Christ!"

"Speak Christian!" yelled Kümmel, meaning that the Span-iard should speak German, not Spanish. "Devil take the buf-foon who invented your barbarous gibberish in the Tower of Babel!"

"Do you recognize him?" Eglofstein asked the dragoon impatiently. "Is he the fellow that stole your purse this morn-ing?"

"Do I recognize him!" Kümmel retorted. "A cap like a stork's nest, a face like a pumpkin and a mouth like a ladle – there isn't another like him in the whole of the army. Come here, my lad, let's take a look at you."

He reached for the torch and looked the Spaniard up and down.

"Captain," he exclaimed, shaking his head in disbelief, "this isn't the man!" He turned to the Spaniard. "May the Devil saddle and ride you: this morning you had only four thieving fingers on your right hand, and now, all of a sudden, you have five."

"Are you sure?" said Eglofstein, barely able to disguise his vexation and disappointment. "Search him – see if he has the money on him."

Dragoon Kümmel felt in the pockets of the muleteer's brown cloak and pulled out a big leather pouch.

"That's it! That's my purse! Do you still deny it, you thieving magpie?"

He looked in the pouch but found nothing. All it contained was some garlic and a piece of bread.

"My money's gone!" he bellowed in a rage. "Why should I always be plucked like a goose? Where are my thalers, pray? Did you pour them all down your gullet in a single day?"

The Spaniard stared helplessly at the floor and said nothing.

"Where's my money?" yelled the dragoon. "What did you do, bury it or drink it? If you have a tongue in your head, speak!"

"God has made a scourge for my back," said the Spaniard. "It is His will. What must be, must be."

"Captain," said Sergeant Urban, "this must surely be the same thief that stole one of the colonel's trunks five days ago – the one in which his late wife's silken gowns and chemises were packed."

"Enough, enough!" Eglofstein said hastily. He was alarmed that the sergeant should begin to speak of the colonel and his wife, being afraid that the muleteer might now come out with what he had overheard of our conversation. "Enough! This Spaniard is found guilty of theft. Muster half a dozen men with loaded muskets, Sergeant. Then march him out into the yard and make an end of him."

"And be quick about it!" Günther urged. "I don't care for priests who say Mass too slowly."

"I'll spend only half as long on him as a Mass takes from *introit* to *Agnus Dei*," said the sergeant. He turned to the dragoons who had followed Kümmel downstairs in their eagerness to see what was afoot.

"Fall in!" he commanded. "Prisoner and escort, by the right, quick march!"

"Señor!" cried the muleteer, breaking away from the dragoons. "You're a Christian. Would you send me to my death unshriven?"

Eglofstein knit his brow. He wanted no delay. To allow the Spaniard to speak with another in private seemed dangerous and contrary to all common sense.

"If I must die, let me first confess!" the Spaniard cried, looking distraught. "You believe, like me, in God and the

49

Holy Trinity. For my spiritual salvation's sake, summon the Señor Cura or the Superior of the Convent of Santa Engracia."

"What need of a priest? Make your confession to him," said Brockendorf, pointing to Lieutenant Donop. "He has a bald pate too, and Latin gushes from his mouth like water from a spring."

"Enough!" cried Günther, for whom matters were progressing too slowly. "Take him away, Sergeant!"

"No!" the Spaniard cried, holding fast to the table with both hands. "Let me speak with the Señor Cura. Only for a short while, a few minutes – only for as long as it takes to say a rosary."

That, however, was just what we had to prevent.

"Silence, you thief!" Günther thundered. "Do you think I don't know what accursed lies you plan to whisper in the priest's ear? Sergeant, take him away!"

The Spaniard looked at him, drew a deep breath, and began again.

"Listen to me, señores. I still have one thing left to do in this town. No one will attend to it when I am dead – not unless you let me speak with the Señor Cura. I cannot die before I know that the task has been entrusted to him."

He gazed at us in turn, wiping the sweat from his brow. All at once he was overcome with despair.

"Is there no one here to heed me?" he lamented loudly. "Is there no Spanish Christian here to heed me?"

"Whatever you've left undone, we shall do it for you," said Eglofstein, eager to settle matters. He tapped his riding boot impatiently with his crop. "Well, tell us what's to be done and then be off with you!"

"*You* will do it for me?" cried the Spaniard. "*You?*"

"A soldier must be able to turn his hand to anything," said Eglofstein. "Quickly, say what's to be done. You wish some turnips planted, a roof repaired?"

Again the Spaniard looked from one to another of us, and a sudden thought seemed to strike him.

"You are Christians, señores," he said. "Swear to me by the Virgin and Child that you will keep your word."

"To hell with your formalities!" cried Günther. "We're officers. We shall do what we have promised to do, and there's an end on it."

"Whatever must be done, we shall do in your stead," Eglofstein repeated. "Have you a donkey to sell? Have you debts to collect? What is the task in question?"

Just then the bells of the nearby church began to ring for midnight Mass, proclaiming to the faithful that the mystery of the holy transubstantiation had been accomplished. The wind bore the sound to us through the chill winter air, and the muleteer did as all Spaniards do when they hear the Mass bell ring out: he went down on his knees, crossed himself, and said in a low, reverent voice, "*Dios viene*, God is coming."

"Well," Günther demanded, "what's to be done? Are we to tread a cabbage patch, stick a pig, slaughter an ox?"

"God will tell you," whispered the Spaniard, still deep in prayer.

"Is there flour to be sifted, bread to be baked, corn to be hauled to the mill? Answer, fellow!"

"God will show you," said the Spaniard.

"Don't be a fool," cried Eglofstein. "Answer! Leave God in peace – he knows nothing of you."

"God has come," the Spaniard said solemnly, rising to his feet. "You made a vow and God heard it."

His demeanour had suddenly changed beyond recognition. Gone was the fear he had shown hitherto. No longer a wretched muleteer accused of theft, he stepped up to the sergeant with a proud and dignified air.

"Here I am, Sergeant. Do your duty."

It escapes me how I could have failed at that moment to perceive who had fallen into our hands, or how I failed to discern the nature of the task bequeathed us by our doomed prisoner. We were all of us blind and had but one thought in mind: that the man who shared our secret must be silenced for ever.

At a nod from Captain Eglofstein I went outside to see that the execution proceeded in a swift and orderly manner. The snow, which lay half a foot deep, muffled the footsteps of the marching soldiers. The courtyard was faintly illumined by a full moon.

The soldiers formed up in line abreast and loaded their muskets. The Spaniard beckoned me over.

"Hold my dog, Lieutenant," he said. "Hold him fast till it's done."

From where we stood it was possible to see the dark vineyards and the hilly, moonlit fields that lay beyond the town wall. Mulberry and fig trees loomed above the snow with their naked branches outstretched. Far to the west, the horizon was fringed with a dark, menacing shadow: the distant oak forests in which lurked our foe, the Tanner's Tub, and his hordes.

"Grant me one last look at the countryside, Lieutenant," said the Spaniard. "This is my land, my native soil. It is for me that those fields turn green, for me that those vines bear fruit and those cattle bring forth young. Mine is the soil that the wind caresses, and mine are the fields that receive the snow and rain and dew from heaven. Mine is all that stirs between those furrows and all that breathes beneath these roofs – mine is all that this sky encompasses. You are a soldier, Lieutenant. You cannot truly understand what it means to say, '*My* land, *my* native soil.' Stand aside and give the order!"

Six shots rang out. The dog howled and tugged madly at its collar. I let the beast go, took the torch from the sergeant's hand, and lit the dead man's face.

The Marquis of Bolibar had resumed his former appearance. Death had broken the mould he had enforced upon his features while playing the part of a muleteer for our deception's sake. His face, as he lay there now, was just as I had seen it that morning: proud, motionless and awe-inspiring, even in death.

The soldiers shovelled away the snow and set about burying him. I walked slowly back across the courtyard to the house. All at once I saw quite plainly what had happened, and what a strange and devious course the Marquis of Bolibar had taken. While leaving his house in secret that morning, he must have encountered Perico the waggoner, who was just making off through the woods with his stolen thalers. He had exchanged clothes with Perico, and his face, which was so mysteriously subject to his will, had taken on the waggoner's features. Thus disguised, he had entered the town incognito to put his plans into effect. And then, without warning, he had found himself as securely incarcerated in the role of a thief as he would have been in a prison cell. Unable to slough off that role without betraying his true identity, he was compelled to play it to the end and suffer a death intended for another.

It was while all these thoughts were passing through my mind that I came to a sudden halt in the snow and smote my brow, for I now grasped the significance of the curious oath he had made us swear. Unheeded by anyone, with death staring him in the face and enemies on every side, the Marquis of Bolibar had entrusted us with the fulfilment of his task: we ourselves were to give the signals that would spell our own destruction.

I felt disposed to laugh at the stupidity of this notion, but my laughter was still-born. The dead man's words still rang in my ears: *Dios viene.*

God had come . . . A shiver ran through me, together with a dread of something that could not be put into words — something that loomed before me as dark, menacing and fraught with danger as the gloomy shadows of those distant oak forests.

I re-entered the sweltering room, which was thick with wine fumes and tobacco smoke. Günther and Brockendorf, their quarrel forgotten, were peacefully sleeping on the floor side by side. Donop sat perched on the table with the Marquis's dagger in his hand, examining the fine workmanship of the carved hilt. Eglofstein was standing in the middle of the room with Captain de Salignac, who had a vociferous and wildly gesticulating figure by the collar and was pushing the fellow ahead of him.

"Eglofstein!" I called. "It was the Marquis of Bolibar you ordered to be shot."

I had expected my announcement to be greeted with surprise, delight and jubilation, but the only response was a bellow of laughter.

"*Another* Marquis of Bolibar?" cried Eglofstein. "How many

53

of them are roaming the streets tonight? My friend Salignac has caught one too."

He pointed to Salignac's prisoner. I could not discern his face, for it was hidden behind one of those black silk handkerchiefs with which married men in Spanish towns disguise themselves when pursuing their nocturnal amours.

"Comrade Salignac," he said mockingly, "you've bought yourself a donkey at a horse fair. I advise you not to hang the worshipful alcalde of this town on our very first day here. We may have need of him."

GERMAN SERENADE

We could not forbear to burst out laughing when we saw that our unhappy prisoner was none other than His Portliness the alcalde of La Bisbal. So uproarious did our laughter become that it roused Lieutenant Günther, who got to his feet, rubbed his eyes, and yawned. Brockendorf slumbered on, snoring fit to blow the door off its hinges.

"What is it?" asked Günther, sleepily smoothing down his hair.

The alcalde pursed his mouth into a sour smile at our boisterous hilarity. He twisted his cap in his hands, half incensed, half abashed, with the look of one who has swallowed mouse dirt instead of aniseed candy.

"Señores," he said, "there are nights when we, too, like to tear a bed-sheet other than our own."

One could see, as he looked at our laughing faces, what an effort it cost him to master his annoyance.

"There are women in our town far lovelier than the ladies who lean at night against the pillars of the colonnades in the Palais Royal," he proclaimed, clearly as proud of the fact that his town vaunted such beauties as he was of having travelled so far afield. He was almost as much at home in Paris, he implied, as he was in La Bisbal.

"I've yet to see many choice morsels in your streets," Eglofstein said scornfully.

"Coarse bran, coarse bran!" the alcalde exclaimed. "What you have hitherto seen, señor, is fit only for the likes of us. For officers and gentlemen such as you, I know of some fine white flour." He shut his eyes and smacked his lips, chuckling.

"White flour indeed!" sneered Donop. "White lead, more like. The women smear their wrinkled cheeks with it, and underneath they look like unshaven ox-hide – I know that trick of old."

"Shame on you, señor!" said the alcalde, looking affronted. "If you once set eyes on the girl I have in mind, you would find neither white lead nor any other substance on her cheeks. Monjita is barely eighteen years old, but the menfolk are after her like meadow frogs after a red rag."

"Here with her, then!" yelled Brockendorf from his corner, wide awake in a trice on hearing all this talk of women. "Eighteen, eh? That fires my blood like water on unslaked lime."

"Who is this Monjita?" Eglofstein asked disdainfully. "A tailor's daughter? A wig-maker's trollop?"

"Her father, señor, is a nobleman – one of those that are respected by all as persons of quality, yet are so poor that they don't possess an undarned shirt to their name. Times are hard, and he cannot afford to pay his rent and taxes. He will esteem it a great honour if Your Excellencies find his daughter worthy of their attention."

"What trade does he follow?" Donop inquired. "If it puts no bread on his table, why doesn't he abandon it?"

"He paints pictures," the alcalde explained, "– pictures of emperors and kings, prophets and apostles, which he hawks at the church door by day and in taverns by night. He's exceedingly skilful – he can paint everything, man and beast alike. St Rochus he depicts with a dog, St Nicasius with a mouse, and Paul the Hermit with a raven."

"And his daughter?" asked Günther. "She may well be no older than seventeen, but the girls hereabouts are like our German bagpipes at that age: they squeal if you so much as touch them."

"His daughter," said the alcalde, "is well-disposed toward Your Excellencies."

"Then *allons*, forward! What are we waiting for?" Brockendorf cried eagerly. "I yearn to stew in her little cook-pot."

"But not tonight," the alcalde objected, with an uneasy

glance at the tipsy Brockendorf. "Another time, señores – perhaps tomorrow after dinner. Señor Don Ramon de Alacho will already be asleep at this late hour. For now, I think it would be better if we all retired to bed."

"Have you done?" Eglofstein barked at him. "Yes? Then say no more until you're spoken to. Forward! Take the light and lead on!" He turned to the captain of the Horse Guards, who was pacing restlessly up and down the room. "Will you not come with us, Salignac?"

"I'm waiting for my servant, Baron. He's gone, though I ordered him to stay. Can you tell me where he went?"

"Comrade," said Eglofstein, putting on his cloak, "you were unfortunate in your choice of a travelling companion. Your servant was a thief – he stole a purse from one of my men this morning. He had it on his person, though the thalers had gone."

Salignac was not in the least surprised or taken aback.

"Did you hang him?" he inquired without looking round.

"Wrong, comrade! We shot him outside in the courtyard. The carpenter has promised us a gibbet next week, but not before."

The captain's reply was so strange that I often had cause to remember it in the days to come.

"I knew it," he said. "No man ever lives long who travels a part of the way with me."

So saying, he turned his back on us and fell to pacing the room again.

Wrapped in our cloaks, we left the house and trudged through the snowy streets in the alcalde's wake, each treading in the footprints of the man ahead. We made our way in turn along the Calle de los Arcades, the Calle de los Carmelitas, and the Calle Ancha or "Broad Street", so called because it was wide enough to enable two waggons to pass abreast. The streets were quiet and deserted, for midnight Mass was long over. Having passed the church of Nuestra Señora del Pilar and the Torre Gironella, we came to a square in which stood six lifesize stone statues of saints.

We had walked the whole way in silence, shivering with

cold. The alcalde chattered without cease, pausing every hundred paces to point out various houses with his little silver-knobbed cane. This one, he told us, had been occupied until last year by a man whose cousin was a privy councillor; that one used to be the residence of Don Antonio Fernandez, a justice of the royal bench for India. On this spot, he pursued, the Archbishop of Saragossa had once been obliged to wait for an hour in the heat of the sun because one of his carriage horses had cast a shoe. The little dairy on the right of the church had last year been damaged by a fire in which the owner's wife had perished. The shop over yonder sold all that an officer might require for his comfort.

The alcalde paused to bow and cross himself while passing the church. Loosely affixed to the church door and fluttering in the wind was a sheet of paper. He pointed to it.

"Recorded there and held up to public opprobrium," he said, "are the names of all those citizens who broke their fast or failed to attend confession last Sunday. His Reverence the Cura –"

"Be damned to you and your priest!" Günther snapped at him. "Why keep us standing out here in the cold? Forward! Trot on! We didn't come with you to –"

He broke off, for he had tripped over a dead mule that lay full in our path and measured his length in the snow. Scrambling to his feet with his clothes wet through, he proceeded to heap curses on Spain and its inhabitants, whom he blamed for his misadventure.

"What a filthy, shiftless country! Rusty iron, worm-eaten timber, bug-ridden beds, streets thick with dung, fields knee-deep in weeds!"

"Look at that Spanish moon," Brockendorf chimed in. "It's out of kilter too, the daft thing. Last night it was as thin as pickled herring, and now it looks as plump as a porker."

Meantime, we had at last reached the house of Don Ramon de Alacho, Monjita's father. A squat building of neglected appearance, it stood in the square across the way from the six stone saints.

Günther seized the door-knocker and beat a tattoo.

"Hey, there! Open up, Señor Don Ramon, you've got company!"

All remained quiet inside the house. It had begun to snow again, and our cloaks and caps were turning white.

"Courage, comrade!" said Brockendorf, clapping his hands to warm them. "Break the door down – it won't be as stout as the British lines at Torres Vedras."

"Open up, Señor Slug-a-Bed de Snoreville!" yelled Günther, belabouring the door with the knocker. "Open up, or we'll kick your door and windows in!"

"Open this door, or we'll smash every stove in the house!" Brockendorf bellowed, forgetting that he was on one side of the door and the stoves on the other.

A window in the adjoining house opened and a nightcap appeared. It bobbed back into the darkened room, quick as lightning, and the window shut with a crash. Our snow-mantled cloaks had startled the sleepy citizen, who was doubt-less quaking in his bed and telling his wife that the six stone saints had deserted their pedestals and were noisily disporting themselves outside Don Ramon's door.

Just then an angry voice made itself heard from a window just above our heads.

"Hell's bells and buckets of blood! Who's there?"

"So he can swear like an East India Company deck-hand, can he? Well, so can I!" said Donop. "Open up," he shouted back, "or may you catch the Spanish pox ninety-nine times over!"

"Who's below?" called the voice.

"Soldiers of the Emperor!"

"Soldiers, did you say?" the voice retorted furiously. "Linen-weavers and chimney-sweeps, makers of brooms and cleaners of privies – that's what you are!"

"And who may you be, you miserable cur?" Brockendorf yelled with all his might. "Stop yapping and give us a sight of you!" He was incensed that anyone should have mistaken him for a linen-weaver or chimney-sweep, let alone a member of the guild charged with carrying away night-soil.

"Don Ramon," the voice said in a perceptibly milder tone,

"go down and open the door. I wish to see the fellow that called me a miserable cur."

We heard footsteps inside the house and the creak of wooden stairs. Then the door opened to reveal a misshapen little man with a humpback as big as a molehill in May. He wore leggings of brick-red cloth, cut askew, and a brown woollen nightcap of which the tip hung down over his right ear. The torch in his hand described a fiery arc in the gloom as he gave us a mocking bow, and his shadow was that of a mule stooping to have a camp-kettle strapped to its back.

We followed him upstairs and came first to a room strewn with all manner of painter's materials. In the centre stood an easel bearing a picture of St James of Galicia, the colouring of which was complete save for the ruff and the right arm. The second room we entered was unlit, but a cheerful fire of vinewood burned on the hearth, and a man seated in an armchair was warming his feet at it with legs extended. A pair of Hessian top-boots lay on the floor beside him, and on the table were several glasses, a bottle of wine, and a big tricorn hat _à la russe_.

The man turned his head as we entered, and the firelight revealed, to our dismay, that it was our colonel whom we had serenaded so boisterously from below. Now that we were upstairs, however, it was too late to take to our heels.

"Well, come in," the colonel called. "Which of you is the dog-fancier?"

"Eglofstein," I heard Donop whisper behind me, "you must be our spokesman – he esteems you highly."

Eglofstein stepped forward and bowed. "Colonel," he said, "I beg your pardon, but none of this was meant for you."

"Not meant?" exclaimed the colonel with a resounding laugh. "Eglofstein, I can well believe that you would sooner be anywhere than here at this moment. Amid the pepper trees of Java, eh? Gathering cinnamon in Bengal, perhaps, or in the Moluccas, where the nutmegs grow. Brockendorf, who's the cur now, I or someone else?"

Short-tempered as a rule, and prone to ungovernable outbursts of fury when plagued by one of his migraines, the colonel was tonight in such high spirits that we took advantage of his good humour.

"Colonel," said Eglofstein, pointing to Brockendorf, who stood there with the impenitent air of Barabbas in the Easter Play, "you must make allowances for him. He's not only a fool but blind drunk to boot."

"He lacks *bene distinguendum*," Donop added in Brockendorf's defence.

"Come here, little mirror-gazer!" called the colonel, taking a pinch of snuff from his coat pocket. "Feast your eyes on the man who aspires to lead his colonel around on a leash."

At the other end of the room stood a bed, and hanging on the wall beside it were two pictures of the Virgin, a small vessel filled with holy water, and a looking glass. Standing before the latter with her back to us, tidying the artificial flowers in her hair, was a girl in Spanish costume, the black velvet bodice of which had bows and ribbons adorning every seam. She now walked lightly over to the colonel and put her arm around his shoulders.

"This is Captain Brockendorf," the colonel told her, "the man who called me a cur. See how he stands there, the drunken sot, big as an ox and proud as Goliath. He eats hens and ducks alive."

Brockendorf bared his teeth, glowered at the colonel, and said nothing.

"He's an able soldier, though, as I saw for myself at Talavera," the colonel added after a moment, and Brockendorf's face brightened at once.

"Neither a chimney-sweep nor a cleaner of privies!" he growled. Appeased, he began to stroke his enormous, pitch-waxed moustache and cast ardent glances at Monjita and the wine.

The colonel was more talkative, in his present merry mood, than I had seen him for many a long day.

"Eglofstein, Jochberg!" he sang out. "Come here and take a glass with me. Günther! Man, why stand there like a votive candle?" He filled his glass. "Damn these Spanish thimbles! Oh, for my grandfather's great, big, German catechism glass!"

61

We went to the table and toasted him. He drew Monjita to him and contentedly stroked his red moustache.

"Tell me, Eglofstein," he said with a sudden stirring of emotion in his voice, "is she not the living image of my dead Françoise-Marie? Her hair, her brow, her eyes, her walk! How could I ever have dreamed that I would rediscover the wife God wrested from me, here in this Spanish rat's nest?"

I stared at Monjita in surprise, unable to discern any of these several respects in which the colonel supposed her to resemble his late wife. Although her hair was of the same coppery hue as Françoise-Marie's, and although the conformation of her brow bore a vague resemblance to that of our erstwhile mistress, her general appearance was that of a wholly different person. The others, too, seemed surprised by the colonel's remark. Eglofstein smiled, and Brockendorf gaped at Monjita open-mouthed, like Tobias' fish.

"Come here, you of the burning eyes," said the colonel, taking Monjita by the hand. "You're to have some fine clothes from Paris, did you know that? I have a quantity of them in my baggage." He forbore to tell her that it was his late wife's wardrobe he carried around in his trunks and chests. "Chocolate will be served you in your bed every morning."

"But you must soon take the field again," Monjita said softly, "and God alone knows when you'll return. What will become of me while you're gone?" It was the first time we had heard her speak, and sure enough, her voice was that of our dead beloved. A thrill of joy and melancholy ran down my spine, for Françoise-Marie had once said the same words to me with the same note of sadness in her voice. That, I suspect, was the moment when we first fell prey to the delusion that afflicted us all in the days to come: the belief that we had truly rediscovered Françoise-Marie in Monjita. It was a delusion that caused us to vie bitterly for possession of her, forget the dictates of honour and duty, and contend with one another in a spirit of hatred, jealousy, and murderous passion.

"What?" cried the colonel, dealing the table such a blow with his fist that the wine bottle fell over and the array of pots

62

and pans on the wall danced a jig. "You shall go wherever I go, and be damned to it! Massena never takes the field without a woman – he sends to Paris for another actress every six months."

"An actress?" Eglofstein shrugged disdainfully. "Most of them are merely six-groschen whores from the *petites maisons* in St Denis or St Martin, and when he tires of them he bequeathes them to his aides."

"His aides, eh?" the colonel exclaimed, eyeing Eglofstein with dark suspicion. "I have other bequests in store for *my* aides. They're to inspect their soldiers' cartridges, boots and knapsacks daily. Which reminds me, Eglofstein: have you detailed men to fell timber and fetch water tomorrow? I intend to keep you on your toes, just you wait and see!"

He was quite another man from that moment on: irascible, moody, and brusque of manner. Donop and I unobtrusively retired to the other room, where we found our portly friend the alcalde examining the half-finished St James of Galicia in company with humpbacked Don Ramon of the brick-red leggings.

"Your saint's erudition is plain to see," the alcalde was saying. "I once knew a man who claimed that St James spoke Latin in his mother's womb, but the fellow was a heretic and burned as such."

"In his lifetime," said Don Ramon, "the saint was more learned than handsome. He had a greater abundance of warts on his face than the city of Seville has church spires, but I've painted only two of them. Women are loath to buy a saint with a warty face."

"Don Ramon," I broke in. "You've sold your daughter to an old man. You ought to be ashamed of yourself."

Don Ramon laid aside his brush and looked at me.

"The Señor Coronel saw her at Mass and pursued her," he said. "He has promised her happiness, as people call it. She's to have fine bedlinen of Holland cloth. He'll give her a carriage and pair and a coachman, and she'll ride to Mass in style every morning."

"Is there nothing you wouldn't sell for doubloons?" Donop

asked heatedly. "I'll wager you'd cut Judas down from the gallows for thirty pieces of silver. What must your St James think of such a transaction?"

"St James dwells in heaven, but I have to live in this merciless world," the hunchback said with a sigh. "I tell you, señor, and the alcalde here will testify on my behalf: it has not been easy to provide myself and my daughter with a morsel of bread each day."

"But you're a nobleman, Don Ramon," Donop raged. "Where's your integrity? Where's your sense of honour?"

"Young sir," said Don Ramon, "believe me, if this war lasts much longer, all integrity will be blighted and all honour rancid."

The colonel was now dismissing the rest of the company in the inner room.

"Eglofstein," I heard him say, "parade the men at eight. Drill them in loading the mules till nine, then have them carry bales of straw and hay to the stables. I want a calash outside this house at ten."

Eglofstein clicked his heels.

"And now, be off to your quarters. Toss a couple of billets into the stove, down a glass of mulled wine, and then pull the blanket up to your chin, eh?"

We bade him good night and went downstairs. Once outside the door, Brockendorf refused to take another step.

"I must go back," he said. "I'll wait till the colonel's gone. I must join her upstairs – I've serious matters to discuss with her."

"Come on, you fool!" hissed Eglofstein. "If you don't, the colonel will notice and turn spiteful."

"Why the devil did we come too late?" Günther complained. "God, how beautiful she is! She has Françoise-Marie's hair."

Overwhelmed with disappointment, we all went our way in sullen silence – all, that is, save Eglofstein, who hummed cheerfully to himself.

"You simpletons!" he said at length, when we were a pistol-shot from Don Ramon's house. "Think yourselves lucky! Our colonel has acquired another wife. If she really resembles his first in every way, as he believes, will he be able to keep her to himself?"

We paused and looked at each other, all with the same thought in mind.

"It's true!" said Donop. "Did you see how the girl caressed me with her eyes when I took leave of her?"

"And me!" Brockendorf exclaimed. "She gazed at me as if to say . . ."

Brockendorf had forgotten what her gaze was intended to convey. He yawned, turned, and directed a lovesick glance at Monjita's window.

"All she possesses is a pretty face and a fine figure," said Günther. "I'll warrant she won't be too unkind when she learns that I've eight Carolingian thalers sewn into my coat collar."

"Long live our colonel and his new wife!" cried Eglofstein. "We'll soon be leading our former life again in *floribus* and *amoribus* – am I right, Donop?"

We shook hands and trudged back to our billets through the deep snow, each of us afire with the hope that he would be Monjita's first choice. It was an eternity before I got to sleep, for Günther, with whom I shared my room that night, insisted on rehearsing the speech he proposed to make Monjita in Spanish. "Fair damsel," he declaimed before the mirror, gesturing like an inferior play-actor bestriding the stage, "God save your soul! I lay my heart at your feet, señorita!"

TROUNCED

For the next few days we toiled away at our duties – at drilling and riding, improving the earthworks, and inspecting the men, stables and billets. Günther and Brockendorf devoted their leisure hours to playing cards at "The Blood of Christ", an inn where decent wine and a warm room were always to be had, and filled it with the clamour of their altercations. Donop and I, who went riding almost daily, brought back partridge, quail, and, on one occasion, a hare. We were cautious the first time, keeping close together and not venturing more than half an hour's ride from the outermost defences. Later, when we found the roads safe and the peasants everywhere at their work, men and women alike, we became bolder and extended our forays far beyond the villages of Figueras and Truxillo.

Of the guerrillas we saw no sign whatever. Such was the peace that reigned in field and vineyard, and such were the courtesy, candour and lack of hostility with which the villagers greeted us, that the region seemed quite innocent of rebellion and ambuscade. The cruel and fanatical Tanner's Tub might never have existed.

Having read all that the ancients had committed to writing since the time of Aristotle, Donop never tired, during these excursions, of telling me how closely the Spanish countryside still resembled the descriptions of it recorded by Lucan in his account of Cato's journey to Utica. The way in which women pounded their sodden laundry on riverside stones had remained unchanged for over two thousand years, he said, and every passing ox-cart filled him with delight because it so vividly recalled the copperplate illustrations of such conveyances in his edition of Virgil's *Georgics*. According to the writers of old, he assured me, the countryside hereabouts was carpeted in summer-time with rosemary and lavender, sage and thyme. He accosted everyone we met on the highroad, whether shepherd, farm-hand, or wood-cutter, but failed to elicit any botanical information because he carried the Latin, but not the Spanish, names of all these plants in his memory.

I had not seen Monjita again since the night we encountered our colonel at her father's house. It seemed that the priest, in response to a request from the colonel, had called on the humpbacked painter the following morning. Some hours later a calash had driven up and conveyed Monjita to the Marquis of Bolibar's town house. This building, which boasted two Saracens' heads over its portal and was situated in the Calle de los Carmelitas, had been chosen by the colonel as his headquarters. The ground floor was given over to the guard, the top floor to Eglofstein's orderly-room.

The inhabitants of La Bisbal, modest, humble folk who earned their daily bread by cultivating olives or vines, dealing in grain or dressing coarse wool, were at first surprised and disconcerted by Monjita's change of abode. In the course of time, however, they welcomed it, feeling highly flattered and honoured that the choice of so senior an officer should have fallen on a neighbour's daughter known to them all since her childhood. Although there had previously been a few disaffected townsfolk who eyed us with contempt 'twixt cloak and hat-brim and secretly called us godless heretics whose extermination would be a meritorious act, all the faces we now encountered were amiable and contented or, at worst, simply curious. What was more, their priest assured them from the pulpit that the Spanish and German nations were on friendly terms – indeed, that they had, to their common renown, been allies since the time of Emperor Charles the Fifth.

Donop and I rode up and down the Calle de los Carmelitas, evening after evening, showing off our horses' voltes and halts, but never once did we set eyes on Monjita. Nothing stirred behind the barred windows, and the Saracens' stone faces gazed mutely down on us from above the door.

Toward noon on the Sunday after Christmas, Eglofstein came to my room to accompany me to dinner, for we were always invited to join our colonel's table when resting in quarters on the Sabbath.

We went downstairs and out into the marketplace, which was thronged, as ever on Sundays, with market women trying to sell us eggs and cheese, bread and fowl, and beggars holding out the grimy effigies of sundry saints for us to kiss. The crowd thinned beyond the church of Maria del Pilar. Eglofstein was in the best of spirits.

"All's well," he announced, slapping the side of his boot with his riding crop as he went. "Things are better, in fact, than I expected. Saracho has the patience and stupidity of a sheep. He hasn't budged – he's lying low and waiting for the signals. Well, he'll continue to wait for as long as I please."

He chuckled softly to himself.

"The house in the Calle de los Carmelitas is being closely guarded," he said, more to himself than to me. "That man Salignac knows his business. He stands guard there, peering at all who approach like the Devil sifting souls. If His Lordship the Marquis of Bolibar wishes to sneak inside and kindle his mouldy straw, he'll have to transform himself into a mouse or a sparrow."

"The Marquis of Bolibar is dead," I broke in, "as I already told you."

Eglofstein paused and turned to stare at me.

"Jochberg," he said, "I credit you with more intelligence than most. How in God's name did you contrive to get drunk so early in the day?"

"The Marquis of Bolibar is dead," I repeated, stung by his imputation, "and you yourself had him shot. We must have been blind not to recognize him at once on Christmas Eve."

"You seriously expect me to believe," cried Eglofstein, "that that filthy Beelzebub of a muleteer, the one that stole Kümmel's thalers, was a cousin of the King of Spain?"

"Yes, Captain, he was. He lies buried beneath the snow, and his dog still roams near the guard post and leaps up at me whenever I approach."

Eglofstein paused again and knit his brow.

"Jochberg," he said, "I know that it has always been a favourite pastime of yours to arouse my ire by contradicting me. You always know better than the rest. If someone says 'sweet', you say 'sour'. If I were to say 'sparrow', you would say 'finch'."

He relapsed into sullen silence, and we walked on side by side for a while.

"I interrupted you, Captain," I said at length, hoping to placate him. "You were about to tell me your plans."

"Ah yes, my plans," he said, and his face brightened in an instant. "Well, as you know, we're expecting a consignment of powder, shot and shell. Our stock of ammunition has been depleted by these latest engagements – severely depleted, Jochberg – but the convoy has already passed the village of Zarayzago and will be here three or four days hence."

"Unless Saracho . . ." I began.

We had come to the "Blood of Christ" inn. Standing outside its door in the wintry sunlight, dripping with melted snow, was a carved wooden figure of St Antony, a saint much revered in Spain and more often invoked there than all twelve Apostles put together. Eglofstein paused with his hand on the latch and turned to me.

"The Tanner's Tub?" he said. "He'll have to let the convoy pass, for he mustn't make a move before the Marquis of Bolibar signals to him by kindling that straw. I myself shall give the said signal in three or four days' time. Once the convoy is safe within these walls, I shall lure Saracho and his men out of their holes as village boys lure crickets, and that'll be the end of the guerrillas in this part of the world."

He flung open the door and shouted into the tap-room.

"Brockendorf! Günther! Are you coming? You know the colonel: keep him waiting for his dinner and he'll confine you to quarters."

Brockendorf and Günther emerged red in the face, one with wine, the other with a gambler's excitement. Günther was cock-a-hoop, Brockendorf as phlegmatic as he always was when not actually drunk.

"Well," said Eglofstein, "which of you won the other's boots? What did you play, 'Thirty-One'?"

"We played 'Lansquenet'," Günther replied, "and I won."

St Antony was holding a slip of paper in his hand, a printed announcement to the effect that Mary had been truly immaculate when she conceived Our Lord. Günther, having removed this, gave him the knave of diamonds to hold instead, and the saint, as forbearing and longsuffering in effigy as he had been in his lifetime, retained the playing card between his fingers.

"Günther," Brockendorf said in his measured way, "at Barcelona, where some felons were marched to work past my billet each morning, I once saw a card-sharper whose face bore a strong resemblance to yours."

"And I," Günther retorted hotly, "saw a thief dangling from a gibbet in Kassel whose nose was as flat as your own."

"Sometimes," said Eglofstein, quite straight-faced, "Nature indulges in the strangest whims."

The four of us set off together.

"He had the king of spades in his hand," Günther pursued, as hotly as ever. "He played it, thinking himself sure to win, and said 'Take that!' And so it went on, thrust and parry, queen of hearts, knave of hearts, back and forth. In the end I played the ace of hearts, called 'Trounced!', and he was beaten."

He turned to Brockendorf and bellowed the word exultantly in his face.

"Trounced, Brockendorf, did you hear? Trounced!"

"Be first with her by all means," Brockendorf growled as he strode along. "She'll notice soon enough that you're not the man for her. Your slow-match peters out too soon, my lad."

Eglofstein looked at the pair of them and whistled softly to himself.

"What did you play for?"

"For the right to be first with Monjita," Brockendorf replied.

"I thought as much," said Eglofstein, chuckling.

"Brockendorf met her in the street this morning," Günther announced. "She made an assignation with him for tomorrow, after Mass, but he lacks the necessary *belair* – he would have choked the well for the rest of us. Now I shall go in his place. I know how the women hereabouts should be courted in Spanish."

Eglofstein turned to Brockendorf, his eyes alight with curiosity.

"Is it true you spoke with her?"

"Yes, and at some length," said Brockendorf, smiting himself on the chest.

"What did you say to her?"

"I told her point-blank that I was in love with her, and that she alone could help me in my hour of need."

"And she? What was her answer?"

"She could not converse with me in the street, she said, because that would be thought unseemly in La Bisbal, but I was to call on her tomorrow after Mass. She had pins and lye in plenty at home."

"Pins and lye?"

"Yes, I had vowed to eat pins and drink lye for love of her."

"Tomorrow, when the colonel has gone riding," said Günther, "I shall pay her a visit."

"Do that!" Brockendorf gave a thunderous laugh. "Go by all means. Swallow the pins and lye yourself!"

"Günther," said Eglofstein, "you and Brockendorf may fancy yourselves the only players in this game, but have a care: I, too, hold some trumps in my hand."

"But the lead is still mine," Günther drawled spitefully. The pair of them, Eglofstein and Günther, eyed one another with the cold and hostile air of duellists preparing to settle matters at dawn.

By now we had reached the colonel's residence. Outside the door we saw Captain de Salignac furiously engaged in driving away a number of beggars who, it being Sunday, had gathered at the Marquis of Bolibar's house to get their customary dole of soup and peas cooked in oil.

"What are you doing here, you rogues, you scoundrels, you drunken wine-bibbers?" Salignac roared at them. "Be off with you! I'll let none of you past this door!"

"Alms, sir!" the beggars cried in a ragged chorus. "Alms, if

71

you yourself hope to receive God's mercy! Have pity on the poor! Glory to God on high! Feed the hungry!"

"You see?" said one of the wretches, thrusting his mutilated arm in Salignac's face. "Like you, I have been afflicted with a divine misfortune."

Salignac retreated a step and called out the guard. At once, two dragoons emerged from the doorway and put the beggars to flight with a shower of blows. Even as he ran, one of the fugitives turned and called over his shoulder.

"I know you, cruel man!" he cried. "Christ has already punished you once for your hardness of heart. You have no more hope of eternal bliss than the beasts of the field!"

The captain watched him go without expression. Then he turned to me.

"Lieutenant Jochberg," he said, "you are the only one of us to have seen the Marquis of Bolibar. Did you recognize him in one of those wastrels? I think it very likely that he will endeavour to steal back into his house in some such disguise."

I strove to explain that the beggars had merely come for their Sunday alms, but he did not hear me out. Instead, he began to lay about a peasant who, half hidden behind a mule laden with firewood, had been gazing into his face with mingled curiosity and fear.

"What are you doing here, you stubborn rogue?"

Trembling all over, the peasant put a hand to his brow, lips and breast in turn.

"Leave me be, Jew," he entreated. "Acknowledge the Cross!"

We laughed despite ourselves on hearing the captain called a Jew, but Salignac seemed not to have heard. He fixed the man with a menacing, suspicious gaze.

"Who are you? What's your business here? Who sent for you?"

"I bring firewood from the forest for the Señor Marques, Your Eternity," the peasant said haltingly, crossing himself again and again as he bestowed this singular title on the captain.

"Take your firewood and go to the Devil – let him stoke the

fires of hell with it!" Salignac roared, and the peasant turned
and ran off down the street, terrified out of his wits, with the
mule cavorting madly after him.

Salignac drew a deep breath and rejoined us.

"An arduous spell of duty, this. It has been the same since
daybreak. You, Eglofstein, sitting snug in your orderly-room,
can count yourself lucky –"

He broke off, for just then a peasant drove up with a waggon-
load of maize straw, and Salignac, suspecting him to be another
Marquis of Bolibar in disguise, showered the unfortunate man
with curses and imprecations.

We left them to it and set off up the stairs.

In the dining-room above we found Donop in conversation
with the priest and the alcalde, who had likewise been invited
to dinner. Donop was dressed to the nines: he wore his best
breeches, his boots were carefully polished, and the black stock
at his throat was knotted in keeping with the latest fashion.

"She will be at table," he announced, walking over to us
with an air of mystery.

"I doubt it," Günther retorted. "Our Colonel Vinegar-Jug
keeps her tethered like a nanny-goat."

"I met her on the stairs," said Donop, "and she was wearing
a gown of Françoise-Marie's, the white muslin '*à la Minerve*'.
I felt I was looking at a tombstone come to life."

"She wears Françoise-Marie's clothes every day," Eglofstein
told us. "The colonel wishes her to resemble his first wife in
each and every respect. Believe it or not, she has had to learn
to distinguish between all the *vins de liqueur* – to tell a Rosalis
from a St Laurens, for example. Now he's busy teaching her
to play cards: *ombre, piquet, petite prime, summa summarum*."

"I can think of other games I should like to teach her," said
Günther. He began to laugh, but at that moment the door
opened and Monjita herself came in with the colonel at her
heels.

We fell silent and bowed – all save the priest and the alcalde,
who were standing at the window with their backs to the
door, unaware of the colonel's arrival. They continued their

conversation, and the alcalde's voice could plainly be heard in the general hush.

"My grandfather met him here in this very town, fifty years ago, and he's just as the old man described him: for ever vehement and choleric, his face the colour of death and his brow encircled by a bandage that conceals the fiery cross."

"His portrait hangs in the cathedral at Cordoba," said the priest, "and beneath it are the words: *Tu enim, stulte Hebrææe, tuum deum non cognovisti*, which is to say, 'Thou foolish Jew, thou didst not –'"

He, too, became aware of the colonel's presence and fell silent. After a general exchange of salutations we all took our places at table, I between Donop and the priest.

Monjita, recognizing Captain Brockendorf as the man with whom she had spoken that morning, smiled at him, and I, as I watched her sitting beside the colonel in the white, high-necked muslin gown we all knew so well, was truly tempted to believe, if only for a moment, that she was the Françoise-Marie whose memory I had never been able to banish.

Donop seemed to feel as I did, for he left his plate untouched and never took his eyes off her.

"Donop," the colonel called across the table as he tempered his Chambertin with water, "you or Eglofstein must play us something on the pianoforte after dinner. Your health, Señor Cura!"

"Donop," I whispered to my day-dreaming table companion, "the colonel was addressing you." He gave a start and sighed.

"Ah, Boethius!" he said softly. "Ah, Seneca! Great philosophers though you were, how little have all your writings availed me!"

The meal proceeded, and I remember its course as if it were yesterday. The lofty windows facing me afforded an extensive view of snow-mantled hills on which isolated bushes stood out like dark shadows. Jackdaws and ravens fluttered across the fields, and in the distance a peasant woman rode her donkey toward the town, a basket on her head and a child on her lap. None of us guessed what a transformation would overtake the peaceful countryside that very day, nor could we know that we were enjoying the last harmonious hour we were ever to be granted within the walls of La Bisbal.

Günther, seated beside the alcalde, regaled him with a loud and boastful account of his feats of arms and his travels in France and Spain. My neighbour on the right, the priest, while applying himself with alacrity to the food and wine, lectured me on matters of which he assumed me to be ignorant – for instance, that the region was very hot in summer, that the countryside abounded in figs and grapes, and that fish, too, were plentiful by reason of the sea's proximity.

All of a sudden Brockendorf sniffed the air several times, smote the table with his hand, and let out an exultant cry.

"The dish has conceived and brought forth a roast goose – I can smell it from here!"

"Damnation," said the colonel, "you guessed it. Very perceptive of you."

"It comes at a blessed hour, does the goose," Brockendorf declared, brandishing his fork. "Let us greet it with a *Con quibus* or a *Salve regina!*"

"Hush, Brockendorf," said Donop, as embarrassed on the priest's account as the rest of us. "Forms of worship are no fit subject for mockery."

"Keep your homilies to yourself, Donop," Brockendorf growled. "You're no theologian, God knows." The priest, however, had understood none of this but "*Salve regina*".

"The Bishop of Plasencia," he said, helping himself to a drumstick from the dish, "the Most Reverend Don Juan Manrique de Lara, grants forty days' worth of indulgences to all who say a *Salve regina* before Our Lady's statue."

"Don't stint yourself, sir," Brockendorf benevolently urged the alcalde. "When one dish is empty, another will be brought."

"Our beloved Maria del Pilar," pursued the priest, "is admired and revered throughout the world, having accomplished as many miracles as the Maria de Guadalupe or the Virgin of Montserrat. Why, only last year . . ."

The words stuck in his throat, together with a morsel of roast goose, and his startled eyes sought those of the alcalde.

Both men stared in alarm at the door. Following the direction of their gaze, I gathered that the cause of their sudden consternation was Captain de Salignac, who had just entered the room.

Salignac removed his cloak, bowed to the colonel and Monjita, and regretted that the importance of his guard duties had been such as to delay him. Then he sat down at table, and I saw for the first time that his tunic was adorned with the cross of the Légion d'Honneur.

"You won your cross at Eylau, I believe?" said the colonel. He signed to Monjita to serve him, and we all marvelled at her slender hands and graceful movements.

"Yes, at Eylau – the Emperor himself pinned it to my chest," the captain replied, and the eyes beneath his bushy eyebrows shone. "I had returned from delivering a dispatch to find the Emperor at breakfast, hurriedly drinking his chocolate. '*Grognard*,' he said to me, 'bravely ridden, my old *grognard*. How fares your horse?' I may be an old soldier, Colonel, but I swear my eyes grew moist at the thought that the Emperor could still find time, in the hurly-burly of battle, to inquire after my horse."

"All I fail to understand about your story," said Brockendorf, wiping his mouth, "is that the Emperor should have taken chocolate with his breakfast. Chocolate tastes of syrup and is sticky as pitch. It also leaves grounds between the teeth."

"I've spent two years in the field and taken part in seventeen battles and engagements, among them the assault on the Lines of Torres Vedras," Günther said resentfully, "but I've yet to be awarded the Légion d'Honneur because I wasn't serving in the Guards."

"Lieutenant Günther," Salignac replied with a frown, "you have been at war for two years and seen action seventeen times. Can you guess how many battlefields *I* have trodden – battlefields unknown to you even by name? Can you guess how many years before your birth I first wielded this sabre?"

"You heard that?" the alcalde whispered to the priest, and he drew the sign of the cross on his forehead with trembling fingers.

"Lord have mercy on the luckless man," said the priest, casting his eyes up to heaven.

"What foolishness to drink chocolate!" Brockendorf persisted. "A good beer soup, a brace of sausages well stewed in gravy, and a tankard of ale to go with them – that's *my* favourite breakfast."

"Have you often seen the Emperor at close quarters, Salignac?" asked the colonel.

"I have seen him at work in a hundred guises. I have seen him dictating letters to his secretaries while pacing his room. I have seen him studying maps and engaged in geographical computations. I have seen him dismount from his charger and lay a gun with his own hands. I have seen him listening to petitioners with knitted brow and galloping across the battle-field, head bowed and grim-visaged, but I was never so filled with a sense of his greatness as when I once entered his tent and saw him lying exhausted on his bearskin, stirring restlessly in his sleep as he dreamed with twitching lips of battles to come. He seemed to me then to resemble none of the generals or conquerors of our own day. I was reminded by his awesome appearance of that murderous old monarch –"

"Herod!" exclaimed the vicar. "Herod!" groaned the alcalde, and they both stared at Captain de Salignac with horror written on their distracted faces.

"Herod, yes," said Salignac, "or Caligula." And he poured himself some wine.

"The Emperor," Donop said slowly and thoughtfully, "is leading us along a road that traverses vales of misery and rivers of blood, but its destination is liberty and human happiness. We must follow him for want of any other road to take. Having been born into an ill-starred age and denied peace on earth, we can only hope for peace in heaven."

"There you go again, Donop," said Brockendorf, who was peeling himself an apple. "That's as pretty a speech as any uttered by a mendicant nun after Confession."

"What do I care for peace?" Salignac exclaimed with sudden vehemence. "War has been my lifelong element. Heaven and its perpetual peace are not for me."

77

"I know it," wailed the alcalde.

"We know it," groaned the vicar. *"Deus in adjutorium meum intende!"* he added in a low voice, folding his hands and composing his tremulous lips.

The colonel had meanwhile declared the meal at an end, so we all rose to our feet. Salignac threw on his cloak and strode downstairs with a jingling of spurs. The priest and the alcalde gazed fearfully after him until he was lost to view. Then the former tugged at my sleeve and drew me aside.

"That officer who took his leave a moment ago," he said, "– ask him if he was ever in La Bisbal before."

"In La Bisbal?" I replied. "When would that have been?"

"Fifty years ago in my grandfather's time, when the great plague was raging," the alcalde interposed, as if it were the most natural thing in the world.

I burst out laughing at this nonsense, at a loss to know how to answer. The alcalde raised his arms in entreaty and the priest, with a terrified gesture, urged me to be silent.

Donop, who was conversing with Günther, never took his eyes off Monjita.

"Never have I seen such a resemblance. Her figure, her hair, those movements . . ."

"The resemblance will not be perfect," Günther interrupted him in his arrogant way, "until I've taught her to whisper 'Till tonight, my dearest' when she bids me adieu."

"Günther!" the colonel called suddenly from the other end of the room.

"Here, sir," Günther called back, going over to him. "What may I do for you?"

I saw the two of them exchange a few words. A moment later Günther returned, his lips set in a stubborn line and his face as white as the wall.

"I am to hand over my command to you," he hissed at me, "and ride this very day to Terra Molina with letters from the colonel to General d'Hilliers. So *that* is Eglofstein's ace of trumps!"

"You may be sure the letters are extremely urgent," I said, glad that the colonel's choice had not fallen on me. "I'll lend you my Polish galloper. You'll be back within five days."

"And tomorrow you'll call on Monjita in my place, eh? You're in league with Eglofstein, just as I suspected. You and Eglofstein: rancid butter on mouldy bread!"

I did not answer, but Brockendorf stepped in.

"I have your measure, Günther," he sneered. "You're afraid – you can already hear musket balls whistling past your ears."

"Afraid? I would charge a battery of howitzers head-on, and you know it."

"The colonel respects your fine horsemanship," said Donop.

"Enough of your parrot's chatter!" Günther burst out. "Do you imagine I didn't see Eglofstein at table with the colonel, whispering in that furtive way? He wants me a hundred miles from here on Monjita's account, and I won't forget it – be damned if I will! Eglofstein is for ever spying. If two people stand talking together, he sidles up behind them like a customs inspector."

"What else can you do?" said Donop. "You have your orders from the colonel, and no amount of cursing and swearing will change them."

"Well, I won't go, not in a month of Sundays! A thunderbolt can bury me ten thousand fathoms deep before I quit the field in favour of the rest of you!"

I nudged him in the ribs, for Monjita, accompanied at the pianoforte by Eglofstein, had just begun to sing.

The very first notes transfixed me with melancholy, for I had often heard Françoise-Marie sing the same aria. Like Monjita, she would stand there with her dainty head bowed and a wealth of red-gold hair cascading over her rounded, girlish shoulders, surreptitiously smiling across at me, and I would thrill to the blissful recollection that it was only yesterday I held that trembling body in my exultant hands, and only yesterday that I had rapturously smothered that melodious mouth with kisses. And a sudden thought entered my head and filled it to the exclusion of all else. No, I told myself, it cannot be otherwise: when I take my leave of Monjita, bending low over her hand, she will secretly whisper to me, as Françoise-Marie was wont to do, "Till tonight, beloved!"

79

All at once Monjita broke off in the middle of a phrase and gave the colonel an imploring glance. He went over to her and tenderly stroked her russet hair.

"This is the first time she has sung it for company," he told us, "and only the beginning has lodged in that little head of hers."

"Monjita has a fine voice," the priest said, venturing out of his corner. "She has sung in our church on feast days, together with a licentiate whom the Señor Marques de Bolibar employed for a while in his library. He now holds a good curate's post in Madrid."

"That name again!" exclaimed the colonel. "One hears no other in your town all day long. Where is this Marquis of Bolibar? Where is he skulking? Why cannot I see him face to face? I have good reason to seek his acquaintance."

It would have been wiser to remain silent, but my secret was giving me no peace.

"Colonel," I said, "the Marquis of Bolibar is dead."

Eglofstein frowned and got up from the pianoforte.

"Jochberg," he said in an irritable tone, "do you truly mean to weary us yet again with your foolish fairy-tale?"

"It is as I say: on Christmas Eve, when I was commanding the gate guard, I had the Marquis of Bolibar shot by my men."

Eglofstein shrugged. "A figment of his overheated imagination," he said, turning to the colonel. "The Marquis of Bolibar is alive and will, I fear, give us a deal of trouble yet."

"Well," said the colonel, "be he alive or dead, we know his plans and have taken all steps necessary to prevent them from being put into effect."

"And I tell you, and I stand by what I say," I cried, stung by Eglofstein's mocking and supercilious manner, "that the man is dead and buried. We're battling with a ghost, a bugaboo, a chimæra."

Just then the door burst open and Salignac entered, his face even paler than the bandage around his head. He stood there sabre in hand, all breathless from running up the stairs, and his eyes sought the colonel's.

"Colonel," he panted, "was the signal given on your orders?"

"The signal?" exclaimed the colonel. "What do you mean, Salignac? I gave no order."

"Clouds of smoke are rising above this house! There's straw smouldering on the roof!"

Eglofstein squared his shoulders, white to the lips.

"This is his doing. We have the man at last."

"What man?" I exclaimed.

"The Marquis of Bolibar," he replied, leaden-tongued.

"The Marquis of Bolibar?" Salignac cried in an extremity of agitation. "Then he must be in the house. No one has left by the door!"

He rushed out, and we heard a slamming of doors and a thunder of footsteps as his dragoons charged wildly through the house, searching every room, passage and stairway.

Günther's voice broke the spell. "Colonel," he said, "is it not time you gave me those letters for General d'Hilliers?" He was lolling against the wall with his hands behind his back, smiling, and it occurred to me that I had not seen him in the room for some minutes.

"Too late," the colonel said darkly. "Another hour, and the town will be encircled by guerrillas. You would never get through their lines. The convoy is lost."

"So the child is still-born," drawled Günther, and his eyes shone with the malign exultation of a Judas Iscariot. "Many thanks for the offer of your Polish horse, Jochberg. I shall not be needing it now."

"And the worst of it is," Eglofstein said gloomily, "we have no more than ten rounds per man. Do you still maintain that the Marquis of Bolibar is dead, Jochberg?"

I alone heard the muttered response that came from where Günther was standing: "Trounced!"

WITH SAUL TO ENDOR

On Tuesday morning I left the town to take up my duties in the Sanroque outwork, for we had begun to strengthen the ramparts and entrenchments, and two semicircular outworks with counterscarps and wide ditches were already half completed. The lines were jointly manned that day by Brockendorf's company and a half-battalion of the Prince of Hesse's Own, which had been sent to reinforce us not long before. My dragoons, whose turn it was to do duty in the town itself, were patrolling the streets.

While passing the presbytery I came upon Thiele, my corporal, seated on the ground with a battered camp kettle between his knees, whistling "Our Cousin Mathies", a marching song, as he hammered out the dents with a mallet.

"Lieutenant," he hailed me from across the street, "hell has sprung a leak since yesterday, and demons by the bushel are roaming abroad."

It was the guerrillas of whom he spoke. Fearing to lose my way unaided in the maze of entrenchments that lay between the walls and the Sanroque outwork, I bade him accompany me. He shouldered his mallet and fell into step beside me, swinging the camp kettle.

The appearance of the town had altogether changed overnight. Despite the fine winter weather, the marketplace was deserted and the streets were devoid of the many water-carriers, fish- and vegetable-sellers, muleteers and beggars who ordinarily went about their clamorous business at this hour. Apart from a few old crones who flitted across the street from doorway to doorway, hurriedly and with anxious faces, the townsfolk were hidden away indoors.

Yet there was life and noise enough. Dispatch riders galloped unceasingly to and fro between the outworks and the colonel's headquarters, rumbling powder waggons overtook us, and mules laden with provisions and entrenching materials filed past. The Hessians' surgeon had installed himself in a hollow beyond the town gate and was leaning against an ambulance waggon, smoking his pipe and awaiting the first of the wounded.

"The night pickets have already had a brush with the enemy," Thiele told me as we went our way. "They sent back three prisoners with their report. All three looked as if they were newly landed from Noah's Ark. How comes it that all these guerrillas have the faces of monkeys, mules or goats?"

After thinking awhile, he himself supplied an explanation for this singular phenomenon.

"Most likely," he said, "it comes of their partiality for eating corn cobs and acorn mash, victuals such as we feed to our beasts at home. They're quiet now, but an hour ago you could have heard them wailing piteously. They stood in a circle round their officers and chanted their morning prayer. It sounded like a hymn to Behemoth, the demonic patron of blasphemy and cattle fodder."

He spat contemptuously on the ground. By now we had reached the Mon Cœur lunette, which was enclosed by a palisade. The Hessian grenadiers lay stretched out in the trench on their kitbags and knapsacks. The officers on duty, Captain Count Schenk zu Castel-Borckenstein and Lieutenant von Dubitsch, two figures in pale blue tunics with tiger-skin revers, were conversing at the mouth of the lunette. The hauteur with which they returned my formal salute stemmed from the longstanding enmity between their regiment and ours, its origin being a parade in Valladolid at which the Emperor had omitted to bestow so much as a glance on the Prince of Hesse's Own.

We traversed the redoubt and, by way of the Estrella curtain, reached the first outwork, where I sent Corporal Thiele back. I found Brockendorf's men hard at it, for this part of the fortifications was barely half finished. Some of the men were revetting the walls with gabions and fascines, others improving the embrasures in the parapet, and others at work on the penthouse roof. Donop, spade in hand, was supervising the laying of a mine to be set off in the event that the colonel should order this part of the defences to be demolished. His breakfast of bread and a bottle of wine lay beside him on the ground, together with a treatise by Polybius on the art of warfare in the ancient world.

"Jochberg," he called, resting his spade against the wall, "you can go home again. Günther has taken over your duties today."

"Günther on duty in my place?" I said, surprised. "That's the first I've heard of it."

"He volunteered," said Donop. "What's more, you owe your day of leisure to Monjita."

Laughingly and a trifle maliciously, he recounted the lamentable outcome of Günther's visit to Monjita. It seemed that he had called on our colonel's lovely mistress punctually after Mass the previous day. He apologized for bringing her no flowers. Had it not been winter, he said, he would have presented her with a bouquet made up of roses for ardent love, of blue forget-me-nots for true remembrance, of delphiniums, the flowers of St George, and of tulips and violets, whose romantic significance I forget.

He had then declared his love and assured her how heartfelt it was, and Monjita sent for iced water and chocolate and heard him out with a smile, for Günther's polished phrases seemed to please her. She asked him if he had ever been to Madrid and if what her father said was true, namely, that all the people one saw in that city's streets were either English cobblers or French barbers.

Rather than pursue the subject of Madrid, Günther began to speak of the colonel, whose dearest wish, he said, was to father a son and heir. If he got one, he would assuredly make Monjita his wife.

Monjita's eyes lit up at these words. She proceeded to question Günther about the colonel's late wife and asked if he had known her. He must tell her all about the dead woman, she insisted, for she wished to become like her in every respect but had much to learn.

"One learns so little from our Spanish books," she said with a sigh. "When a king was born and when he was baptized, which princess he married and who arranged the match – things of that sort, nothing more . . ."

Günther reverted to the colonel's desire for a son. Then, his conversation with Monjita having already taken so intimate a turn, he went a step further. If only she would avail herself of his services, he said, he himself could readily assist her in this matter.

Monjita looked puzzled, for his meaning had at first escaped her, so Günther repeated his proposal in plain language.

At this she rose without a word, turned her back on him, and went to the window. Günther, who assumed her to be thinking the matter over, waited patiently for a while. At length, however, he rose and, hoping to further his cause, kissed the nape of her neck.

She swung round and glared at him with flashing eyes. Then she swept past him and out of the door.

Günther, all the more piqued and disappointed for having felt so confident of success, lingered alone in the room for an hour or thereabouts. At last, when the hour was up, Monjita reappeared.

"What, still here?" she said, her anger unabated.

"I was waiting for you."

"I have no wish to see you any more. Go!"

"I shall not go until you have forgiven me."

"Very well, I forgive you, but now go quickly. The colonel has returned."

"Then give me a kiss in token of your forgiveness."

"You must be mad. Kindly go!"

"Not until –" Günther began.

"For the love of Christ, go!" Monjita whispered urgently, but just then the door opened and the colonel appeared on the threshold. He stared in surprise, first at Günther and then at Monjita, who was standing by the door, pale and distraught.

"You wished to see me, Lieutenant Günther?" he said.

"I wished," stammered Günther, "– that is to say, I came to report before taking up my duties."

"Did you not find Eglofstein in his office? What post have you been assigned?"

"The Sanroque outwork," Günther said swiftly.

"Very good," said the colonel. "Be careful of the guerrillas."

Günther hurried from the room and stormed downstairs. In the street he met Donop and, still seething with fury like a saucepan on the hob, told him of his unsuccess.

"And that," Donop said in conclusion, "is how you came to be relieved of your duties and why Günther must perform them in your place. You owe it to Monjita, with whom I hope to have better luck than Günther, whose glib demeanour so ill conceals the clumsy oaf beneath."

Günther had yet to appear, but Eglofstein was standing behind the breastwork with Brockendorf in attendance and his glass trained on the guerrillas, large numbers of whom were swarming about near the village of Figueras and on the farther bank of the river Douro. Their long grey cloaks were visible to the naked eye, and one could even, through the telescope, discern the red cockades in their caps.

"They possess all manner of artillery," said Eglofstein, lowering the glass. "Twenty-four-pounders, for example, and there's a ricochet battery to the right of that church in Figueras. However, I hope they'll give us time enough to complete our work on the fortifications."

"Guerrillas' artillery!" growled Brockendorf. "Does it scare you? I know those cannon – they're carved in wood and mounted on ploughshares instead of gun-carriages."

Eglofstein shrugged his shoulders and said nothing, but Brockendorf fell to cursing.

"Devil take the colonel! Does he intend yet another interminable delay before he gives the order to attack? Grenades and grapeshot, comrades! I've blithely endured all the trials and tribulations of battle, but this endless waiting drives me mad."

"The colonel," said Eglofstein, "has weighed his reasons well. I'm acquainted with his strategic plans, and –"

"Strategic plans?" Brockendorf said furiously. "Any fool can make strategic plans. You and I could do so quite as well as the colonel, and with less sweat and cogitation."

"General d'Hilliers is over yonder," said Donop, who had joined us and was pointing westward with his spade. "If the rebels give him time to attack, his advance guard will suffice to settle the issue."

"Spare us," said Brockendorf, looking him up and down. "Go teach your recruits to clean their muskets."

"Well, Brockendorf, tell us *your* strategic plan," Eglofstein said scathingly. "Don't leave your gun half-cocked, fire away!"

"My plan," said Brockendorf, stroking his moustache with a ferocious air, "is as follows: grenadiers on the right, skirmishers on the left. By the right and left, deploy! Present your muskets, take aim, fire! How else, pray, should a grenadier earn his daily groschen and two pounds of bread?"

"What then?" asked Eglofstein.

"What then? Why, I should relieve those brigands of a brewer's copper, a hand-mill, and hops and barley sufficient to make five barrels of beer when we're safe back home in our billets come nightfall."

"Is that all?"

"No, by the saints! I should see to it that you got your bag-wig, Eglofstein." That, it seemed, was the sum total of Brockendorf's strategic plan.

"You've forgotten one thing, Brockendorf," Eglofstein remarked, "and that's the order: 'Sound the retreat! Fall back, men! Run for your lives!'" His voice sank to a whisper. "We have only two packets of cartridges per man, didn't you know?"

"All I know," Brockendorf said sullenly, "is that I shall never win myself a Légion d'Honneur in this hell-hole, and that all my money is gone. The very thought of my impoverished state is a torment."

"Ten live rounds per man, that's the extent of our reserves," Eglofstein said in a low voice, looking round to satisfy himself that none of the rank and file could hear. "God alone knows how, but the Marquis of Bolibar must have learned that a consignment of sixty thousand cartridges was on its way to us."

"I spent all my pay at Tortoni's in Madrid," Brockendorf lamented. "There were some excellent stewed kidneys and a kind of little pie filled with mackerel roe, a delicacy unequalled anywhere else in the world."

"But how the devil did he get into the house and out again?"

"Who?" asked Donop.

"The Marquis of Bolibar," Eglofstein exclaimed. "I own I can find no answer to that question."

I could have answered his question with ease, but I preferred to keep what I knew to myself.

"In my opinion," Donop said firmly, "the Marquis is still hiding somewhere on the premises. How else could he have kindled the straw at precisely the right moment? You disagree? In that case, crack the nut for me."

"Salignac combed the whole house for him," Eglofstein objected. "He left neither cat nor mouse undisturbed. If Bolibar had been lurking on the premises, Salignac would have found him."

"Strangely enough," said Brockendorf, "my men think it Salignac's fault that the convoy fell into rebel hands. I don't understand it. They say the regiment's fortunes have worsened since Salignac joined us. All the heart has gone out of them."

"The same may be said of the peasants and the townsfolk of La Bisbal," Donop chimed in. "They all go in mortal dread of Salignac. It's droll to see how they scuttle round the nearest corner and cross themselves whenever he comes along. They behave as if he had the smallpox or the evil eye."

Donop's remark, coupled with that of Brockendorf, had greatly perturbed Eglofstein.

"Is this true?" he demanded. "They cross themselves? They give him a wide berth?"

"Yes, and the womenfolk shoo their children indoors when they see him coming."

"Brockendorf," Eglofstein said after a brief silence, "do you

88

remember when the Polish lancers mutinied at Vitebsk?"

"I do. They demanded good bread and no more floggings."

"No, you're mistaken. The Polish lancers banded together one night, crying out that their commander was accursed and that his presence was to blame for an outbreak of plague in the regiment. The Emperor had thirty of them shot as an example – they were made to draw strips of black and white paper from a bag. And who was their commanding officer? Salignac!"

We stood there in astonished silence. It was almost noon by now. A puff of warm wind sped across the fields, and the air seemed to herald a thaw. From around us came the clang of spades and shovels and the gentle whisper of subsiding soil.

"Gentlemen," said Eglofstein, squaring his shoulders with an air of decision, "I have harboured a certain notion for days, but this morning I find it nagging at me more insistently than ever. Can I trust you? May I speak my mind? Will you be discreet?"

We gave him our word and fixed him with a curious, expectant gaze.

"Knowing me as you do," he began, "you must be familiar with my contempt for every kind of foolish superstition. I care not a fig for God or the saints or the Auxiliaries or any of the other mythical creatures that inhabit the imaginary realm known as Paradise. No, Donop, don't interrupt me! Like you, I have read Arndt's *Wahres Christentum* and Brockes' *Irdisches Vergnügen in Gott*. They contain many fine phrases, but there's nothing of substance underlying them."

Donop shook his head. We were standing so close together that the white horsehair plumes on our helmet bosses met and mingled.

"I pour scorn," Eglofstein pursued, "on the dotards who drivel about inauspicious quarters of the sky, or inimical constellations, or the pernicious influence of Venus, the sun or the Triangle. As for the women hereabouts, who will read any man's hand for half a quarto and, with earnest mien, trace the course of his life-line, heart-line and luck-line, all such goings-on are either nonsensical or fraudulent, however seriously the Spaniards may take them."

"Go on, go on!" Donop urged him.

"But one thing I do believe. Laugh if you will, but I believe in it as firmly as any devout Christian believes in transubstantiation: there are those who are harbingers of destruction. They bring ruin and disaster wherever they go. Such people exist, Donop – I know it for a fact, even if you laugh and call me a phantast."

"Why should I laugh? There comes a time when everyone accompanies King Saul to Endor."

"And that is why I was so startled when Salignac appeared in our midst on Christmas Eve. Not that I showed it, I wished him and his orders in Hades or anywhere but here."

"What's amiss with Salignac?" asked Brockendorf, stifling a yawn.

"Brockendorf! You fought in the Prussian campaign like me – you must have heard of Salignac. I'll tell you what I know of him."

Eglofstein seated himself on an upturned gabion and rested his chin on his hands.

"In December of 1806, Augereau's corps crossed the Vistula at the village of Ukrst. Unopposed by the enemy, the crossing had gone well. Then, just as the last pontoon was casting off, up rode Salignac, who was carrying dispatches from Berthier to the Emperor, and took his place on board. The craft had reached the middle of the river when a stray musket ball struck the helmsman. Panic and confusion ensued. Salignac's horse reared, the boat capsized, and seventeen grenadiers from Colonel Albert's regiment drowned within sight of the entire corps. Salignac alone swam his horse to the farther bank. Those Polish lancers at Vitebsk knew what they were about when they mutinied."

"Do my ears deceive me, Captain?" Donop exclaimed. "Would you really draw conclusions from such a coincidence?"

"*Was* it a coincidence? Perhaps, but the coincidences multiplied. Hear me out."

Eglofstein took a notebook from his pocket and glanced at it.

"What I shall now tell you relates to the destruction of the

16th of Foot in January 1807. The regiment was marching along the banks of the Warta to Bromberg, driving swarms of enemy cavalry before it. At nightfall on January 8th the men bivouacked at a spot protected by trees and clumps of willow. Not long after dawn the regiment was attacked by Prussian hussars. This being an almost daily occurrence, Colonel Fénérol would have beaten them off with little difficulty had he not, for some inexplicable reason, mistaken them for elements of Davout's corps until his men were hand-to-hand with them. Colonel Fénérol fell at the very outset of the engagement, and his fine regiment was cut to ribbons. All this may be well known to you. What you do not know, I'm sure, is that Salignac, with two squadrons of chasseurs from Murat's cavalry, had joined the regiment the previous day, and that he was the only officer who succeeded in fighting his way through to Bromberg. If you call *that* a coincidence . . ."

"But Captain," said Donop, with mounting bewilderment, "there may be the most natural explanation in the world for all you say."

"Then listen to another instance – one that concerns myself. On February 11th of the same year I arrived in Pasewalk and went looking for a billet, for the night was bitter cold and the snow lay two feet deep. In the street I came across Salignac, who was again riding courier and, like me, had yet to find a night's lodging. Such was his reputation in the army, even then, that he was said always to be present when disaster struck and always to escape unscathed. I made some jocular allusion to this, I remember, but he did not reply. In the end we found a corner of a stable unoccupied and resolved to spend the night there.

"At one o'clock in the morning I was roused by an explosion so violent that the ground beneath us shook. A powder mill in the vicinity had gone up, together with half the neighbourhood. The screams of the injured and dying could be heard on all sides. A rafter had fallen on my arm and broken it, but Salignac, quite unhurt and fully dressed for the road, was pacing up and down, weeping."

"Weeping?" Donop exclaimed.

"So I fancied."

"That puts me in mind of something," said Donop, wrinkling his brow. "When I was a child my mother often told me of a man who wept because he was doomed to bring misfortune on the world. Who was it she spoke of?"

"But what alarmed me most," Eglofstein went on, "was that Salignac set off again within the hour. To me, in my bemused condition, it seemed that he had only been waiting for disaster to strike, and that, once it had done so, he was at liberty to ride on and wreak havoc elsewhere."

"The man that wept," Donop repeated slowly, lost in thought, "the one of whom my mother told me – who could it have been? Whoever it was, I've forgotten."

I recalled the singular utterances of the peasant and the beggars and the strange behaviour of the alcalde and the priest at the colonel's table. "Lord have mercy on the luckless man!" the priest had said, gazing distractedly at Salignac, and all at once I remembered Salignac's own words on Christmas morning: how he had muttered, half to himself, that no man ever lived long who travelled a part of the way with him. A thrill of fear ran through me – fear of what, I could not have said – together with an inkling of some weird and age-old mystery. I sensed it only for an instant; then it was gone.

All around me, the grenadiers' spades and shovels and muskets cheerfully reflected the winter sunlight. The church tower rising above the little village of Figueras, the snow-clad branches of the mulberry trees on the far-off hills – everything, even the most distant objects, stood out with crystalline clarity in the brilliant light of that fine winter's day. I continued for a moment longer to sense a hint of what had oppressed me; then it vanished and my spirits were restored.

"The day before yesterday," said Brockendorf, "I mislaid two bottles of claret and one of burgundy. It pays to get to the bottom of things, so I searched the house and found them under my landlady's bed. Salignac bears no blame for that, at least. Claret, I should add, is the meanest, thinnest, most watery stuff in the world, and I drink it only for want of anything else."

Just then, a stream of savage oaths came to our ears from the nearby demibastion. It was Günther, who had made a belated appearance and was urging the grenadiers to work faster. Brockendorf promptly hailed him.

"Günther," he bellowed, "come and join us. Tell us what honeyed words she lavished on you!"

Günther came, looking sullen and resentful. He threw me a venomous glance, I being the one whose duties he had, willy-nilly, to undertake, and sought out a dry place to sit down. Brockendorf went and stood over him, arms akimbo.

"Come now, no secrets. What did she tell you? That you were to visit her again soon? That no one would be more welcome in her bedchamber than you?"

"You're the most garrulous, bibulous dolt of all – that's what she told me," Günther retorted spitefully, and lashed out with his boot at a fieldmouse lying dead in the bottom of the trench, where one of our grenadiers had killed it with his spade.

I saw Captain Eglofstein give an angry frown, for he disliked us to quarrel within earshot of our men. Brockendorf, however, was less aggrieved than gratified.

"Is it true she spoke of me?" he asked with a broad grin. "You mean it?"

"Yes," said Günther, all mockery and malice. "She wants to put you in her herb garden to scare the rabbits away."

"Günther!" Eglofstein interposed. "Kindly address Brockendorf in a more respectful fashion. He was serving with the regiment before you could hold a sword."

"I didn't come here to be lectured," snapped Günther.

"You need a lecture," Eglofstein told him, "– on good manners, to be precise. You're for ever arguing, for ever carping."

Günther jumped to his feet.

"Captain," he said heatedly, "if the colonel addresses me by my rank, I can surely demand the same courtesy from you."

Eglofstein stared at him for a moment.

"Günther," he said, very calmly, "sit down again. Your impertinence is so gross, I find it quite disarming."

93

"That's enough!" shouted Günther, hoarse with rage. "You'll either withdraw that insult, or . . ."

"Or what? Pray go on."

"Or," cried Günther, drawing a deep breath, "I shall compel you to give me satisfaction in a manner that will render you unfit to continue to wear an officer's uniform."

Donop and I opened our mouths to intervene, but it was already too late.

"Very well," Eglofstein said easily, "if you insist." He turned to his orderly, who was seated in the trench not far from us, mending an empty sandbag.

"Martin," he called in a dispassionate tone, "have a brace of pistols and some hot coffee ready at six tomorrow morning."

We were alarmed, knowing that Eglofstein had spoken in earnest. As adept with a pistol as he was with a sword, he had dispatched two opponents and shattered another's arm in the course of the previous year alone.

Günther had turned pale, for although he acquitted himself tolerably well in action, he became unmanned by the sight of a pistol trained on him. Realizing that his quick temper and ill-humour had placed him in an awkward position, he strove to extricate himself.

"Rest assured," he said coldly, "that I shall meet you when and wherever you choose."

"In that case," said Eglofstein, "it only remains for us to make the necessary arrangements."

"Unfortunately," Günther went on, "Soult has forbidden duels in the face of the enemy. I have no alternative, therefore, but to postpone the settlement of this matter until a more suitable time."

We said nothing, for Günther was within his rights. Soult had indeed issued such an order to the officers of his corps some time before. Eglofstein bit his lip and turned to go, but the present outcome was not to Brockendorf's taste.

"Günther," he said, "this whole affair is no concern of mine, nor has Eglofstein requested me to act for him, but the guerrillas are lying low. I hear no shots, I see no movement on their part.

94

They are not comporting themselves like enemies, so to my mind –"

"The guerrillas," Günther broke in, "are only awaiting the Marquis of Bolibar's next signal to storm this outwork. He gave the first on Sunday last, and if the next comes today or tomorrow, as I suspect it will, the first dance will be mine."

I could not but admire his effrontery. We both knew that the Marquis of Bolibar was dead, just as we both knew who had given the signal with the smouldering straw, but he calmly held my gaze, confident that I would say nothing.

Eglofstein shrugged his shoulders and stared past him with an air of contempt.

"If that's how matters stand," said Brockendorf, "I suggest we go back and attend to the inner man. Why wait? The 'Blood of Christ' inn is serving pancakes and fried bacon today, and a brown cabbage soup to start with. Let's be off."

He took Eglofstein by the arm and we walked away, leaving the outwork in Günther's charge.

When we reached the Mon Cœur lunette, which commanded a view of the spot we had just left, Eglofstein suddenly paused, seized me by the shoulder, and pointed.

"Look at him, the cowardly, prating braggart!" he exclaimed, his pent-up anger bursting forth. "First he quakes with fear, and now he seeks to show us what a daredevil he is!"

We could see Günther swaggering up and down the entrenchment as if deliberately courting a hail of bullets from the guerrillas. He knew as well as we that the Spanish musket balls would not carry so far, and that the rebels would not bring their ordnance to bear until they received Bolibar's signal. Eglofstein angrily shook his fist.

"I wish," he said, "that the Marquis of Bolibar would take it into his head to give the signal at this particular moment."

He savoured the thought for a while, chuckling to himself.

"Hell's teeth," he went on, "what fun it would be! Think of it: Günther would be down from that parapet and into the trench quicker than a frog into a pond."

We walked on.

95

"By the way," Donop said casually, "where does the Marquis keep his organ?"

"In the chapel of St Daniel's Convent," Brockendorf replied, "which we've fitted out as a workshop for drying powder and filling shells. I commanded the guard there last night. Pay it a visit if you're so inclined. You could try the instrument for yourself and see if it has a passable tone."

A FORGATHERING OF SAINTS

We left the inn flushed with wine, and, almost before we had
donned our cloaks and set off down the street, fell to arguing
how we should spend the afternoon. Donop, who said he was
very weary, proposed to return to his billet to read and sleep
awhile. Brockendorf suggested that Eglofstein should set up a
faro bank – he had received some inherited money at Perpignan
some weeks before, through Durand's the bankers – but
Eglofstein pleaded that he had no time and must repair to his
office for an hour to attend to the day's business.

Brockendorf, turning peevish, made no secret of his contempt for paper-work in general and the duties of a regimental
adjutant in particular.

"No one," he declared, "could sharpen as many quills in a
day as you wear out in an hour. You fill innumerable sheets of
paper, and all they're good for is grocer's cornets of cinnamon,
ginger or pepper."

"Unless I write out vouchers for you all today," said
Eglofstein, "you'll get no money tomorrow. The paymaster
will give you nothing without my signature."

We walked on, keeping to the middle of the street to avoid
the melted snow that trickled from the eaves. A cat was playing
with a cabbage stalk, patting it back and forth in the noonday
sun. Two sparrows were squabbling over a grain of maize with
ruffled feathers and a deal of angry twittering. Water splashed
over our boots at every step.

At the corner of the narrow lane our path was barred by a
mule which, though handsomely decked out in little bells and
coloured ribbons, the latter being braided with its mane, was

striving to throw off its pack-saddle by rolling about in a puddle of melted snow. The muleteer stood alongside, cursing and cajoling it by turns, thrashing it with his stick and holding dried maize leaves under its nose, calling it the love of his life and an offspring of the devil – in short, doing all he could, for better or worse, to persuade the beast to get up and move on. We watched the spectacle with amusement, while the mule paid as little heed to its master's endeavours as if a flea had coughed or a louse cried murder.

All at once Donop gave an exclamation of surprise, and we saw Monjita, who had failed to notice us, hurrying down a side street.

She had a small basket in one hand and, in the other, the fan with which she was for ever toying. There was a mantilla about her shoulders and a fine silken fillet over her hair. As I watched her tiptoe around the puddles and gather up her gown to avoid them, I fancied for a moment that Françoise-Marie was flitting past in a huff, without bestowing so much as a glance on me, because I had neglected to keep her company for so long.

"She's homeward bound," said Eglofstein, "taking her father whatever is left from the colonel's table. She does so every day, I'm told."

We left the cursing owner of the obdurate mule to his own devices and set off slowly in Monjita's wake.

Delighted that our path should have chanced to cross that of the colonel's lovely mistress, we resolved to visit her father's house and pay court to her on the pretext of examining his pictures and purchasing one of his archangels or apostles.

Brockendorf, who was wary of this plan, uttered threats and reproaches the whole way there.

"I'll tell you this much," he growled. "I'll buy no St Epiphanius or Portiunculus, not even if it's to be had for two groschen. Paintings of saints or pumpkin leaves are all the same to me. You won't catch me out a second time as you did in Barcelona, where I joined you in that wretched tavern for the sake of comradeship and a pretty face. I had to drink up four whole bottles of poor Cape wine by myself, and all because you chose to fall in love with the landlord's niece."

98

He was still grumbling and calling himself the world's most arrant fool for coming with us when we entered Don Ramon de Alacho's work-room.

Peering through the open door into the next room, we saw the object of our visit standing there. She had draped her mantilla over the back of a chair and was busy setting the table with platters of cold meat, bread, butter and cheese. Don Ramon came out from behind one of his paintings, bowed in the ludicrous fashion already familiar to us, and declared himself surprised to see us there.

When we explained that we had come to choose one of his pictures, he welcomed us courteously and with evident delight.

"My house is yours. Remain for as long as you please and make yourselves at home."

There were another two persons in the room – odd-looking figures both. The first, a young man with an artless face, was standing there stiffly with his thin arms raised in entreaty, like a stone seraph, and one could see that the sleeves of his jacket, which were much too short, reached no further than his bony elbows. The old woman seated on a stool beside him was wringing her hands in despair, or so it seemed. Her face was set in a dolorous expression, and she twisted and turned her head incessantly like a scaup-duck.

Don Ramon fetched two of his paintings.

"Here," he said, "you see St Antony surrounded by more than a dozen demons of whom some have assumed the guise of cats, others of bats."

He deposited the picture on the floor and held up another.

"This painting portrays St Clement in the very act of performing a miracle, to wit, curing a splenetic by touching him with his foot."

Brockendorf closely examined St Clement, who was depicted complete with his papal insignia.

"If that's a miracle," he said at length, "I myself am a saint and never knew it till now. I've often performed miracles of that kind. Many's the time I've brought a malingerer to his feet with a hearty kick on the rump."

"It's a good piece," said Don Ramon, "but you can have it for a sum that will cover my expenditure on canvas, oil and pigment with a little to spare."

He brought out the remainder of his paintings, one after another, and we were soon surrounded by a whole congregation of martyrs and doctors of the Church, apostles and penitents, popes and patriarchs, prophets and evangelists. Holding monstrances, chalices, missals, censers, crucifixes and pyxes in their hands, they regarded us with stern solemnity, as if they had fathomed the worldly motives that had prompted us to join their saintly band.

The painter offered to sell Brockendorf a picture of St Leocadia, the Toledan martyr. Depicted on a blue ground, she wore a red robe sprinkled with stars and held an open book in her hands.

"This saint," Don Ramon declared, "has the features of my daughter, who is even now in the room next door, spreading slices of bread with cold meat and cheese. The Señor Coronel keeps a good table and is generous." He raised his voice. "Not too much cheese, my girl! You know it overwhelms the more delicate flavour of the cold roast meat." In the same breath, he went on, "I give all the female saints my daughter's face, likewise the Holy Virgin."

Don Ramon deposited the martyred Leocadia on the floor with the other pictures.

"If you visit the church of Nuestra Señora del Pilar, you will find another painting of mine, a portrayal of the seraphic nun, Theresa, on the right-hand wall behind the second column. That holy woman, too, has my daughter's features – indeed, the resemblance is very marked. It is because the picture shows her wearing the habit of the Discalced Carmelites that the people of this town call my daughter Monjita, or 'little nun', though she received the name Paolita at her baptism."

Brockendorf studied the saints' pictures with a close attention that surprised me.

"Do you also have a picture of St Susanna?" he asked at length.

"This is she, if you refer to the saint who was beheaded in

the time of Emperor Diocletian because she refused to marry his son."

"I know nothing of that," said Brockendorf. "I was speaking of another St Susanna."

"I know of no second saint by that name," the painter exclaimed in great agitation. "Laurentius Surius and Petrus Ribadeira make no mention of any such, nor do Simeon Metaphrastes, Johannes Trithenius and Sylvanus a Lapide. Who was this Susanna? Where did she live, where was she put to death, and which pope elevated her to the rank of saint?"

"What!" Brockendorf said indignantly. "Can you possibly be ignorant of St Susanna? You amaze me. Susanna is the saint whom the two Jews surprised in the bath – it's a well-known story."

"I have never painted that scene, and besides, your Susanna was no saint. She was a Jewess from the city of Babylon."

"Jewess or no Jewess," Brockendorf said firmly, with a very eloquent glance in Monjita's direction, "you should also have painted the young lady as Susanna bathing."

"Don Ramon!" the youth with the upraised arms cried suddenly. "How much longer do you mean to keep me standing here like this for a real-and-a-half? My arms are stiff and crooked enough as it is."

The hunchback took up his brush at once and swiftly vanished behind his easel. For a while, nothing could be seen of him but his brick-red leggings.

"These two persons," we heard him say, "are of service to me in my work. I am painting an *Entombment of Christ*. The young man represents Joseph of Arimathea and this lady here one of the pious women from Jerusalem. Both, as you gentlemen can see, are lamenting the Redeemer's death."

Joseph of Arimathea and the pious woman of Jerusalem bowed to us without in any way relaxing their expressions of bitter reproach and mute despair.

"The señora," Don Ramon pursued from behind his easel, "is an actress of repute. In the morality play we gave last year, here in La Bisbal, she enacted the allegorical figure of Christian

Confession. She won great acclaim and was as conversant with her role as she is with the Paternoster."

"In Madrid," the woman announced, "I have also played queens and ladies-in-waiting."

Brockendorf eyed her closely for a while. Then he said, "I have a pair of woollen stockings spoiled by melted snow. I'm looking for someone to wash them."

"Give them to me!" said the impersonator of queens and ladies-in-waiting, and her features momentarily lost their air of grief-stricken resignation. "You'll have no cause for complaint, I assure you."

Eglofstein, Donop and I had meanwhile retired to the inner room, where Brockendorf joined us. Monjita was still busy setting out dishes and platters on the table. We hemmed her in on all sides like skirmishers surrounding an enemy outpost, and, while Don Ramon diligently painted away at his *Entombment of Christ*, Eglofstein opened the assault on our colonel's mistress.

None of us knew better than Eglofstein how to pay addresses to a woman. He had the knack of using his voice as a master violinist plays his instrument. When he made it tremble and swell, it seemed to convey a passion and emotion which his heart did not truly feel, and there were women enough who fell prey to such empty wiles.

This was the first occasion on which we had been able to speak with Monjita alone, for we had never before seen her unaccompanied by the colonel. Eglofstein began with all manner of little compliments and blandishments which Monjita seemed to welcome, and the rest of us gave him free rein and listened in silence as he pleaded his cause and our own.

He said how happy he was to have met her, for all that rendered his sojourn in the little town tolerable was the prospect of seeing her from time to time.

Monjita smiled with pleasure, and her smile and the way in which her hands toyed with one of the silken flowers in her hair were such that Françoise-Marie seemed to be standing there before my very eyes, as she so often had in the past. And all at once it struck me as bizarre and nonsensical that we should have to expend so many words on winning a woman who had long been ours already.

"Is La Bisbal so wretched a town," she now asked, "that you regret your presence here?"

"No more wretched than any other town in your country, but I miss so many things here: Italian opera, the company of kindred spirits, balls, casinos, sleigh-rides with beautiful women . . ."

Eglofstein paused as if allowing Monjita time to conjure up the diversions of high society – balls, sleigh-rides and Italian opera – in her mind's eye.

"But in your company," he went on, "I can dispense with all such things and am simply content to feast my eyes on you."

Monjita was at a loss how to answer and blushed with delight and confusion, but Don Ramon hailed her from the adjoining room.

"Come now, thank the gentleman for his kindly words, as courtesy prescribes!"

The discovery that Monjita's father had overheard every word of the conversation seemed to fluster Eglofstein and deprive him of his self-assurance. He turned vehement for no reason. When Monjita still said nothing, he addressed her angrily in a much lower voice.

"Can you find nothing to say? Have you no word for me? Very well, look down your nose at me. I'm unworthy of an answer, is that it?"

Monjita shook her head vigorously. She seemed alarmed, perhaps because she feared that she had made an enemy of an officer whom she had often seen conversing privately with her lover.

"You still say nothing," he continued more gently. "I know, you secretly deride the passion which you yourself have kindled in my breast with a single glance from your burning eyes, with one wilful toss of your dainty head, with the unruly ringlet that persists in straying across your marble brow."

"Pay no attention to my hair," Monjita said swiftly. She smoothed it with her hand, relieved that Eglofstein was no longer angry. "It was ruffled by a silly gust of wind as I walked along the street."

Eglofstein, who had not known what else to say, seized upon her allusion to a gust of wind with the dexterity of a juggler wielding his knives at an Ascension Day fair.

"Ah," he exclaimed, "the wind! How jealous I am of the wind, which is permitted, unlike me, to ruffle your hair, caress your cheeks, kiss your lips . . ."

"Don Ramon!" the impersonator of Joseph of Arimathea cried pathetically at that moment. "How much longer am I to stand here? I want to go home."

"Patience! Half an hour more. I must make the most of the time that remains before the light fades."

"What! Will it take so long? A pretty prospect, by heaven, and my mother awaits me at home with a mess of sheeps' tripes she brought from Saragossa."

"Sheeps' tripes from Saragossa, eh?" said the pious woman of Jerusalem, with a sidelong glance at the laden table. "A rare delicacy nowadays."

"Fried in oil with pepper and onions."

"Don't think of sheeps' tripes now, in God's name, nor of pepper and onions!" cried Don Ramon. "Remain as you are and don't move. I paint for the edification of all good Catholics."

Meantime, Eglofstein appeared to have made some progress with Monjita. He had taken her hand and was clasping it in both of his.

"I detect a gentle answering pressure," he said. "The hand that lies in mine is cold and lifeless no longer. May I construe that as a sign that you will grant my heart's desire?"

"Which is?" Monjita asked without raising her eyes to his.

"That tonight you will spend an hour in my arms," Eglofstein whispered.

"That I cannot do," she replied, very firmly, and withdrew her hand.

Seeing Eglofstein's discomfiture, I was overcome with impatience because all his fine words had proved of no avail.

"Listen to me, Monjita!" I cried. "I love you, you know that."

104

Monjita turned to me with a sudden movement of the head, and I felt the heat of her gaze on my brow. She may have smiled in a friendly or mocking way – I could not tell, for I hesitated to look her in the face.

"How old are you?" she asked.

"Eighteen," I replied.

"And already in love? May God preserve you."

Rage and humiliation overwhelmed me at the sound of her soft, merry laughter, for she was no older than I.

"I congratulate you on your good humour," I said, "but you should know that I make a practice of taking by force whatever is denied me on account of my youth."

Monjita's laughter ceased at once.

"Young sir," she retorted, "that would earn you little glory. Although I am not a man, I know full well how to defend myself. But now, enough of this."

Eglofstein gave me a terrible glare.

"Lieutenant Jochberg was speaking in jest," he said, and kicked me on the shin in the lee of the table. "Be silent, you mule, or you'll spoil things for all of us." He readdressed himself to the girl. "Believe me, Monjita, he would never so far forget himself as to force his attentions on a lady."

"A declaration of love should properly be gentle and tender," said Monjita, "but that gentleman, it seems to me, was downright discourteous."

"Stand straight!" Don Ramon adjured his Joseph of Arimathea. "The biblical personage you represent was no hunchback."

"No," I cried, "I'm neither gentle nor tender, for my love is such –"

"I shall never be done if you continue to swallow and cough, yawn and scratch yourself!" Don Ramon exclaimed angrily. "Remain exactly as I showed you!"

"My love is such," I repeated, "that frenzied words are all I can find to express what I have to tell you."

"You're still young," said Monjita, "and love's novitiate is a hard apprenticeship. Doubtless you'll learn how a woman should be treated when you're older."

I looked at her and was incensed no longer, merely astonished that a woman with the voice of Françoise-Marie should have addressed me in so cold and distant a manner.

Brockendorf proceeded to take matters in hand in my place, firmly resolved to bring them to a swift and satisfactory conclusion.

"Why," he asked without ceremony, "would you deny us the little favour you have so readily, willingly and frequently granted our commanding officer?"

"That is an insulting remark."

"Insulting? Far from it. In our country, to make such requests of women is customary, not offensive."

"And in mine," Monjita rejoined curtly, "it is customary to reject them."

Brockendorf, irked that their conversation had failed to take the turn he desired, grew impatient.

"What in the world do you see in the colonel?" he demanded. "He's neither young nor handsome. Be honest: nothing about him is apt to tickle a young girl's fancy. He's tyrannical, waspish, and moody in the extreme. What's more, he suffers from the migraine. Whenever I enter his bedchamber I find it full of pill-boxes, large and small."

"And I thought you were friends of his," said Monjita, quietly and dejectedly.

"Friends of his? Friends are those with whom one would share one's last sip of brandy and morsel of bread. No man is my friend who hides a tidbit from me and keeps it to himself. If that's friendship, my landlady's chamber pot is a priceless goblet!"

"Aren't you afraid that I shall tell him all you've said?"

"Do so by all means!" Brockendorf said brusquely, looking grim. "It's only three months since I left my last man dead on the duelling ground. In Marseille it was, near the Porte Maillot. We fought it out with pistols at six paces." He turned to us. "You remember Captain-General Lenormand, my table companion when I dined with Marshal Soult's staff at Marseille?"

None of us knew anything of this duel. There was no Porte

Maillot in all Marseille, and Lenormand was the name of the humble Rue aux Ours shopkeeper to whom Brockendorf still owed sixty francs for goods supplied: *pâté de foie gras*, a ham, and two bottles of sherry wine.

It was clear that Brockendorf had invented the whole story to frighten Monjita, but we behaved as if we remembered the incident perfectly.

"Yes," said Eglofstein, hurrying to his aid, "except that the lady in question was Lenormand's wife, not his mistress." Musingly, he added, "When a Frenchwoman is pretty, she's pretty with a vengeance."

I had a brief but vivid recollection of the worthy Madame Lenormand. A gaunt, elderly creature with an exceedingly misshapen body, she would come to our billet to demand her sixty francs of Brockendorf every morning save on Sundays, when she went to church carrying a red velvet missal bag.

Monjita gave Brockendorf a look of timid entreaty, and we knew that she would say nothing for fear of endangering the colonel's life.

"He means to make me his wife," she said.

Brockendorf stared at her in astonishment and began to roar with laughter.

"Great heavens! Have the musicians been engaged? Is the wedding cake already baked?"

"What was that?" Eglofstein exclaimed. "His wife, did you say? Has he given you his word on it?"

"Yes, and he gave the Señor Cura fifty reals to cover the cost of the wedding."

"And you believe him? You're deceived. Even if he had a mind to marry you, he could never do so. His noble lineage precludes it."

Monjita looked downcast for a moment. Then she shrugged as if to say that she knew whom to believe and whom not. Don Ramon de Alacho emerged from behind the *Entombment of Christ*, blue paint dripping from the brush in his hand, and addressed us all in a sombre voice.

"No man need blush to wed my daughter, be he count or

duke. She comes of true Christian stock on both her father's and her mother's side."

"Don Ramon," Brockendorf told him, very deliberately, "an ancient patent of nobility carries some weight with me, but if yours attests to nothing save your Christian blood – why, a German innkeeper would wipe his counter with it. In Germany, every cobbler comes of Christian stock."

Joseph of Arimathea threw up his hands in a gesture of dismay and entreaty, the pious woman of Jerusalem shook her head with a look of deepest sorrow, and Don Ramon de Alacho slunk silently back behind his easel.

It was growing dark, and our impatience had mounted as the time went by. Brockendorf uttered a stream of oaths and vowed, loudly enough for Monjita to hear, that none of us would stir from the spot until the matter was settled, even if we had to stand there all night. Donop, who had hitherto left the talking to us, now took the floor.

"It would almost seem, Monjita, that you're truly enamoured of our old colonel."

"What if I am?" she cried fiercely, but it sounded to us as if she was loath to admit, even to herself, that she favoured the colonel over us solely on account of his senior rank, his wealth and generosity.

"The emotion you feel for the old man cannot be love," Donop said quietly. "True love is a sentiment of a different kind, and one with which you are still unacquainted. Love entails secrecy. I shall wait for you tonight, atremble with impatience and frantic with desire, counting the minutes that separate us. And if you steal away to join me, furtively and filled with trepidation, you will look into your heart on the way and discover a new and unfamiliar emotion: *that* is love!"

It was now so dark that I could no longer discern Monjita's face with any clarity, but I heard her laugh – loudly, heartily, and a trifle mischievously.

"Well, I declare! You've converted me. I'm almost curious to become acquainted with the new and unfamiliar emotion you describe. To my regret, however, I've promised to be true to my lover."

Our suspicions should, I suppose, have been aroused by her sudden change of tack and mocking tone, but we were all far too impatient and lovesick to heed them.

"You need not keep that promise," Donop hastened to reassure her, "since you gave it to a man you do not love."

Don Ramon had meanwhile lit a wax candle in the adjoining room, and a slender shaft of light was streaming through the half-open door.

"If it's true, as you say, that a promise given to a man one does not love need not be honoured, you have banished all my misgivings. I undertake to come, and gladly."

There was still a trace of mockery and mischief in her voice, but her face, insofar as I could see it in the candle's meagre light, wore its usual earnest, pensive expression.

"Spoken like a sensible girl!" Brockendorf cried gaily. "And when, fairest Monjita, may we expect you?"

"I shall come after Compline, which will, I think, be over by nine o'clock."

"And which of us will be the lucky one?" Eglofstein insisted eagerly, already jealous of Brockendorf, Donop and myself.

Monjita looked into our faces one by one. Her eyes lingered on mine longer than any, and I felt at that moment as if her eighteen years had at last made common cause with my own.

But she shook her head.

"If I understood you aright," she said, and again I seemed to detect a hint of mockery in her tone, "– if I understood you aright, I shall not experience the novel and singular emotion you have promised me until I am actually on my way to you. That being so, I cannot now tell in whose arms my journey will end."

Opening wide the door to the work-room, she told her father that he had painted enough for today and that supper was on the table.

Don Ramon and the other two were standing before the *Entombment of Christ*, examining the finished picture by candle-light. The artist seemed dissatisfied with his work.

"Where physical posture and facial expression are concerned, my Joseph of Arimathea looks truly pitiable."

"You might have made him a little handsomer," the young man grumbled, plucking at his woefully short sleeves.

"But his gestures are very lifelike," said the impersonator of the pious woman from Jerusalem, and bent a consoling gaze on the painter and his model.

Brockendorf could not forbear to pass judgement himself.

"There are numerous faces in the picture," he said, "and all of them different."

"That is because I always paint from life," Don Ramon told him. "There are bad painters who take the finished works of other masters as their models. If you care to purchase this painting, it will cost you only forty reals. As you yourself have observed, it contains a wealth of figures. You could, if you prefer, have two smaller pictures for the same price. The choice is entirely yours."

"I'll take a brace," said Brockendorf, strongly disposed in the artist's favour by the successful outcome of our venture, "and the bigger they are, the better."

He produced two gold coins whose existence he had artfully concealed from us, for he owed us all money lost at cards. Don Ramon, having pocketed them, thrust the saintly captain and martyr Achatius into Brockendorf's right hand and the Florentine subdeacon Zenobius into his left.

It had meanwhile been agreed with Monjita that the four of us would await her that night at St Daniel's Convent. We went off to buy wine and supper. We were all in high spirits, but Brockendorf's exuberance was such that he hardly knew if he was on his head or his heels. He frightened an old woman by hissing at her like a goose, hid the ladder of a dovecote belonging to a nailsmith in the Calle Geronimo, and insisted on entering the shop of the potter's wife, with whom he was wholly unacquainted, and demanding to know why she had last week deceived her husband with the club-footed clerk of the magistrate's court.

THE SONG OF TALAVERA

St Daniel's Convent, from which the Calle de los Carmelitas took its name, served us as a powder magazine and workshop. The friars, who belonged to the order of Discalced or Barefoot Carmelites, had long since quit the building to fight against us in the bands of irregulars led by Empecinado and Colonel Saracho. The refectory and dormitory, the friars' cells, the cloisters and the great chapter house – all these were now given over by day to grenadiers from our regiment and the Prince's Own, who were engaged in the manufacture and filling of shells, grenades and fire-balls. The chapel, where Brockendorf proposed to spend the night (each of us performed this duty once a week), was strewn with empty powder bags, nails, axes, hammers, soldering irons, box lids, cooking pots, and brightly painted clay pipes discarded by the grenadiers. Lines drawn in chalk on the stone-flagged floor defined the boundaries between the various squads. Discernible on the walls were faded frescoes that depicted the blinding of Samson and the slaying of the giant Goliath, and some grenadier, by adding a moustache and beard, had transformed the shepherd boy David into a likeness of our majestic regimental drum-major. Above the west door, in a carved and gilded frame, hung the portrait of a monk, a handsome man with an episcopal cross on his chest.

The two table braziers, which filled the air with dense clouds of smoke, presented us with a choice between suffocating and freezing. We had finished our supper, and Brockendorf's orderly, who was reputed to be the best forager in the army, was clearing away the remains of our meal.

Across the way from the convent, and separated from it only

by the narrow Calle de los Carmelitas, stood the Marquis of Bolibar's town house. By peering through a gap in the broken chapel window we could see into the colonel's brightly illuminated bedchamber. He was seated on his bed, fully clothed, while the surgeon of the Hessian battalion shaved him by the light of two candelabra placed on the table. His tricorn and a brace of pistols lay on a chair.

The sight of him sent us wild with glee because tonight he would wait in vain for Monjita, who had chosen to come to us instead. We all hated the colonel and feared him at the same time, and Brockendorf gave vent to the rancour in his heart.

"There sits old Vinegar-Jug with his aching head and his shrivelled heart. Will she come ere long, Colonel? Is she already on her way to you? You rejoice too soon, Colonel. There's many a slip 'twixt cup and lip!"

"Not so loud, Brockendorf, he may hear you."

"He'll hear nothing, see nothing and know nothing," Brockendorf crowed triumphantly. "When Monjita comes we'll douse the lights. I shall crown him with the Turkish crescent twice over in the dark, and he'll notice nothing."

"Being as proud as he is of his noble ancestry," sneered Donop, "he can have St Luke's bird added to his coat of arms. That had a pair of horns too."

"Hush, Donop," Eglofstein whispered uneasily, "he has sharp ears – you don't know him." And he drew us away from the window, though the glass was so thick that the colonel could not have caught a single word of what we were saying about him. "He can hear an old crone cough three miles away, and if he loses his temper he'll have you all manoeuvring for three hours in the middle of a ploughed field, as he did last week."

"I could have choked, I was so angry," Brockendorf growled, moderating his voice. "It's high time he bit the dust. The way he routs us out of our billets every two minutes!"

"You're a fine one to talk," Donop protested. "You entered the regiment as a captain, but Jochberg and I! We served under old Vinegar-Jug as officer cadets. A dog's life, it was. Handling currycombs and case-shot every day, carting horse dung out of the stables, toting a week's ration of oats about on our backs . . ."

The church clock of Nuestra Señora del Pilar began to strike. Donop counted the strokes aloud.

"Nine o'clock. She'll be here soon."

"Here we all sit," said Eglofstein, resting his head on his hand, "waiting for one lone girl. There must surely be plenty of girls in this town as beautiful as Monjita if not more so, but I'm dazzled, God help me. I can see only the one."

"Not I," said Brockendorf, and took a generous pinch of snuff. "I have eyes for other girls too. Had you visited my billet on Sunday night, you would have found me with one such: raven-haired, shapely, and quite content with the three groschen I paid her. Her name was Rosina. Nevertheless, I wouldn't say no to Monjita."

He blew some tobacco dust from his sleeve before continuing.

"Three groschen is little enough. The whores at Frascati's in Paris and at the Salon des Étrangers have cost me more in their time."

One of the candles had burned down and was guttering and sizzling. Eglofstein lit another.

"A great deal more," Brockendorf added with a sigh.

"Listen!" Donop said suddenly, and gripped me by the shoulder.

"What is it?"

"Overhead, didn't you hear? There it goes again! It came from the organ loft!"

"A bat!" roared Brockendorf. "He's afraid of a bat, the ninny! Look, it's over there now, clinging to the wall. Donop, I do believe you're trembling. You thought His Lordship the Marquis of Bolibar was seated at the organ and about to give the signal."

He set off up the spiral stairway that led to the organ loft.

"The Marquis must surely know of some secret passage leading from his house to the convent," said Donop. "Sooner or later he'll climb those stairs and give the second signal, just as he gave the first."

113

"Who's afraid of a bat?" Brockendorf called down. He fiddled with the keys and stops but failed to produce a single note.

"Hey, Donop, you learned to play the organ. Come here! Can you find your way around all these flutes and pipes?"

"Brockendorf," Eglofstein commanded, "leave that organ be and come down here!"

"How droll," came Brockendorf's disembodied voice from overhead, and the spacious, lofty chapel lent it a menacing, sinister quality, "– how droll to reflect that if I, up here, were to play 'The Song of the Martinmas Goose' or 'Margrete, Margrete, your shift is peeping out', Günther and Saracho would dance a jig in the outwork over yonder."

Even Eglofstein seemed hugely entertained by Brockendorf's notion. He smote his thighs and laughed till the walls rang.

"That fellow Günther!" he exclaimed. "The windbag, the braggart! If only I could see his face when the bullets start whistling past his nose!"

Meantime, Donop had climbed the stairs as well. He inspected the organ and gave us a painstaking description of its ingenious and unusual design.

It had a wind-chest, pipework, fluework, and reedwork. There were also rows of stops which Donop manipulated and enumerated, each of them having a different name. One was called the principal, another the bourdon or drone, another the spitz-gamba, another the quinte-viola, another the great sub-bass, and yet another the gemshorn.

"Curious names," mused Brockendorf, "and yet, for all these flutes, pipes and oboes, one cannot strike up an air that's fit for dancing, only a wretched 'Benedicat vos'."

"But one *can* play fugues and toccatas, preludes and interludes," said Donop, springing to the defence of his instrument.

"Tread the bellows for me," Brockendorf urged him. "I've a mind to see if I can manage a 'Gloria'." And he began to sing in a raucous voice.

> Our worthy curate, woe, alas
> forgot his Latin during Mass.
> Kyrie eleison!

Donop crouched down behind the corpus and trod the bellows while Brockendorf ran both hands wildly over the keys, and all at once the organ emitted a thin, shrill note like the squeak of a rat. Faint as it was, it startled Donop and Brockendorf and sent them scampering down the stairs as fast as if the Devil himself were at their heels.

"Brockendorf!" roared Eglofstein. "Come down here, you raving lunatic! You've lost your wits!"

Brockendorf stood there panting, still aghast that the organ should so suddenly have come to life and squeaked like a rat.

"I meant to strike up a jig for young Günther," he said. "Like it or not, I was only jesting."

"Spare us any more such pranks, Brockendorf," Eglofstein growled. "We shall be at grips with the guerrillas soon enough, and then you can win your Légion d'Honneur."

We fell silent for a while, clustering around the braziers on account of the cold. Then we heard footsteps in the street.

"Monjita!" cried Donop, and ran to the window. "She's here!"

But it was not Monjita; it was the surgeon, who, having trimmed the colonel's red beard for him, was returning to his billet lantern in hand.

"Compline must be over," said Eglofstein. "What can be keeping her?"

Our legs and fingers were numb with cold. We marched briskly up and down to warm ourselves, arm in arm, and the muffled echo of our footsteps resounded from the chapel's walls.

Again we sought to while away the time with conversation, and Brockendorf and Donop fell to arguing how the friars of the convent had occupied themselves when assembled in their chapter house.

"They would have sat there," Donop opined, "debating at great length whether Christ had a guardian angel and who was the holier, St Joseph or the Virgin Mary."

"Wrong!" said Eglofstein. "You credit Spanish friars with too much erudition. Meat and drink are their true field of study. Any disputations in which they engaged would have concerned the form to be taken by the letters they addressed to the town's wealthy citizens, soliciting lard and butter in the name of their patron saint. You would find scores of such missives upstairs in the Frater Circator's cell."

"Those mendicant friars know how to live," Brockendorf said with an envious sigh. "Whenever one of them comes my way, all twelve pockets of his habit are stuffed with bread, wine, eggs, cheese, fresh meat and sausages – victuals enough to feed a man for a fortnight. The wine is poor, though. Spanish priests drink a wine as black as ink – it agrees with no one but fools like themselves."

He came to a halt and warmed his hairy hands over one of the braziers. The cold had become unbearable without benefit of stove or blanket, and an icy wind was whistling through the broken window. Donop peered down into the street, burning with impatience, but still Monjita failed to appear. Eglofstein stamped each numb and frozen foot in turn.

"I and my half-company," he said, "were once billeted in an abbey at Bebenhausen, a place in Swabia. I've never known better quarters before or since. We drank arrack and Rhenish wine, and both were so plentiful that we could all have washed our hands in them daily. By night we slept on chasubles, but we suffered from the cold, then as now. It was a hard winter, and the frost was such that crows fell lifeless to the ground and church bells sprang cracks. One night we stoked the fire with two worm-eaten choir stalls."

"You must have had to pay my lord abbot a pretty sum when you marched on."

"Pay?" Eglofstein laughed. "Do you suffer the ox to demand his hide back when your boots are full of holes? Pay? Who in Germany ruled the roost at that time? His highness the elector, his lordship the landgrave, his honour the magistrate, his grace the bishop. Everyone presumed to give orders – audit officers and government ministers daily issued decrees and edicts which no one obeyed. Nowadays, of course, it's another matter: only one man rules, namely, Bonaparte, and all our princes and counts and provosts and prelates have to dance – nay, caper like hungry poodles – to his tune." He paused to listen. "That must be Monjita at last!"

"It must be," cried Donop. "I know her step."

Hurrying to the window, all four of us, we saw Monjita flitting along the street like a moon-cast shadow.

"She's a good girl," Brockendorf murmured, quite affected that Monjita should have kept her word, "damned if she isn't!"

"Come away from the window," Eglofstein commanded in an anxious whisper. "And douse the lights, or the colonel may see us."

We blew out the candles and stood waiting in the gloom. Moonlight slanted down through the lofty windows of stained glass, daubing the flagstones with pallid ornaments and curlicues, rings and circles, while the braziers sprayed the darkness with crepitating sparks. In his room across the way, the colonel paced slowly up and down like a priest composing next Sunday's sermon.

Brockendorf, leaning against the table, could not contain his malicious glee.

"Hey, Vinegar-Jug!" he jeered. "Still awake? Has your beloved kept you waiting tonight?"

"Quiet, quiet!" Eglofstein entreated. "If ill luck decrees that he should hear you . . ."

But Brockendorf would as soon have bitten off his tongue as keep his pleasantries to himself.

"Let him hear me and welcome!" he cried. "I'm sorry for the old fool. Tomorrow I'll send him someone in Monjita's place, to wit, the potbellied crone who sweeps the floor of my room each day. Let him console himself with her. She has a body like a whale and a face like a nutshell, but a bundle of gipsy rags is good enough for the likes of him."

All at once the colonel paused and looked toward the door. Brockendorf began to laugh again – immoderately so, because he found it a great joke that we could watch the colonel waiting with such confidence for the mistress we had lured away from him. In lieu of Monjita, he offered to get him all the old women he had ever seen in La Bisbal.

"Heed my advice and go to bed, Vinegar-Jug. You wait in vain – Monjita will not be joining you tonight, but I'll send you the toothless hag that hawks beans and turnips in the street below my window. She would be the proper woman for you – she, or the scraggy old beldam who washes dishes in the tavern kitchen, or . . ."

He fell silent.

The door of the room across the way was slowly and cautiously opened, and the next moment Monjita – young, beautiful, slender, and thirsting for love – flung her arms round the colonel's neck.

None of us spoke a word. The sight of her smote us like a cudgel between the eyes, like a dagger through the heart.

But then it burst forth, the long-suppressed rancour, the chagrin, disappointment and wounded pride that possessed us at the thought that we, not he, had been deceived.

"Coward!" yelled Brockendorf. "Rogue! Poltroon! At Talavera you skulked behind a mule's carcass while we were charging into the grapeshot!"

"Twelve thousand francs of our pay you pocketed, not to mention eight thousand francs for biscuit and salt meat, while we were made to go hungry. The men went into battle without an ounce of bread in their bellies!"

"Had your cousin not been secretary of war to the Prince of Hesse, Marshal Soult would have ripped the epaulettes from your shoulders!"

"How many remounts have you entered in your books twice over, you thief, you skinflint, you brother of Judas?"

We bellowed ourselves hoarse with rage, but the colonel heard nothing. He loosed the silken fillet from Monjita's hair and took her face between his hands.

"He doesn't hear!" cried Brockendorf, almost choking with anger. "But he shall, by God, if I have to rouse all the devils in hell!"

He hammered so fiercely on the window that fragments of glass fell tinkling into the street. Then, leaning far out over the sill and beating time with his clenched fists, he raised his deep bass voice in a raucous rendering of the lampoon against the colonel which a dragoon and a grenadier had composed after the battle of Talavera, and which the soldiers sang when they thought no officer could hear them:

> When our colonel goes to battle
> and he hears the muskets rattle
> and the cannon's voice sonorous
> joins the mortar in a chorus,
> then you'll see him sweat a river,
> pray and blubber, quake and shiver.

Brockendorf paused, breathless and exhausted, but the colonel showed no sign of having heard. He had both arms around Monjita and was holding her close, and we had perforce to look on while she buried her face in his chest with her copper-coloured tresses falling softly over his shoulder.

This spectacle multiplied our hatred a hundredfold and transformed us into demented fools. Blind and deaf to all else, we had but one thought: that the colonel should be made to hear us, and that we must wrest Monjita from his arms.

"Join in, all of you – then he'll hear!" Brockendorf exhorted us, and he launched into the Song of Talavera once more. And we all joined in, bellowing the words into the cold night air with every ounce of strength in our lungs:

> When our colonel goes to battle
> and he hears the muskets rattle
> and the cannon's voice sonorous
> joins the mortar in a chorus,
> then you'll see him sweat a river,
> pray and blubber, quake and shiver.
>
> But when gold o'erflows his pockets
> and his purse is stuffed with ducats
> that by rights belong to others,
> then his pluck he soon recovers!

Suddenly, while we were still singing, Monjita released herself from the colonel's embrace. Going to the Madonna on the wall, she stood on tiptoe and covered its face with her silken fillet as if the Mother of God must not be permitted to see what was about to happen in the room.

At the same moment the colonel blew out the candles. My last sight was of a slender, girlish figure standing before the Holy Virgin – that and the colonel's grotesquely distended cheeks. Then everything vanished: the table, the bed, the two candelabra, the veiled Madonna, the tricorn on the chair – all were engulfed in darkness, yet I seemed to see the shadowy figures of the colonel and his beloved hasten to each other in a transport of desire and become one.

At that, we were overcome with fury. We forgot the town's predicament – forgot that Saracho and his guerrillas were only awaiting the signal to attack. Beside me I heard an oath so blasphemous that my blood ran cold, together with a cry like the howl of a rabid dog. An instant later I saw Brockendorf and Donop racing up the wooden stairway to the organ.

One trod the bellows while the other played. The organ blared forth, and the Song of Talavera filled the chapel from crypt to vaulted ceiling. All four of us joined in – I saw Eglofstein beating time like a madman – and the organ drowned our voices.

> But when gold o'erflows his pockets
> and his purse is stuffed with ducats
> that by rights belong to others,
> then his pluck he soon recovers.
> Oh you Judas, oh you varlet,
> in your helmet plumed with scarlet!

All at once I came to my senses. My face broke out in a cold sweat, my knees trembled, and I asked myself again and again what we had done. And still the organ continued to thunder "Oh you Judas, oh you varlet!"

And I seemed to see Death seated above at the organ with Satan treading the bellows for him, while down below, in the middle of the nave, standing tall and terrible against a shower of incandescent sparks from the braziers, loomed the shade of the Marquis of Bolibar, beating time to our funeral hymn with wild and triumphant gestures.

Then, quite suddenly, all was still. The organ fell silent, and nothing could be heard but the wind whimpering and moaning in the broken window. The four of us stood huddled together, shivering with the cold, and beside me I could hear Brockendorf's hoarse breathing.

"What have we done?" Eglofstein groaned. "What have we done?"

"What possessed us?" gasped Donop. "Brockendorf, it was you that cried, 'Donop, up to the organ!'"

"I? Not a word passed my lips. It was you, Donop, that bade me tread the bellows."

"I did no such thing, as I hope for eternal salvation. What evil spirit drove us to it?"

A window rattled across the street. Hurried footsteps and confused shouts filled the air. In the distance, a drummer beat the alarm.

"Outside!" hissed Eglofstein. "Outside, quickly! No one must find us here."

We fled across the chapel's echoing flagstones, overturned the table as we went, plunged down passages and up flights of steps, tripped over powder kegs, fell headlong, picked ourselves up, ran for our lives.

Just as we reached the street, the first salvo came thundering out of the mountains.

FIRE

I leaned against a wall for a spell, struggling to catch my breath, mortally weary and shivering with cold. Little by little it came to me where I was and what was happening around me.

Hadn't Brockendorf vowed that the colonel should hear us, even if he roused all the devils in hell? Well, the colonel had heard us at last, and by God, all hell had broken loose.

The rebel artillery sent an endless succession of fire-balls and howitzer shells raining down on La Bisbal's streets and buildings. The environs of the town hall were partly in flames, fire had gained a hold on the flour mill beside the bridge over the Alcar, dense clouds of black and noxious smoke belched from the dormer windows of St Daniel's Convent, and two tongues of flame were darting heavenward from the roof of the presbytery.

The bells of Nuestra Señora del Pilar and the Torre Gironella pealed forth, sounding the tocsin. Detachments of grenadiers ran aimlessly through the town exchanging shouted injunctions to attack, open fire, charge, form squares, attempt a sortie. Here and there one could glimpse the pale and terrified faces of townsfolk hurrying through the streets, burdened with their belongings, to take refuge in the cellar of some neighbour's house that had so far escaped the conflagration.

The colonel dashed out of his quarters half-clad, calling repeatedly for Eglofstein and his servant, but no one heeded or recognized him. He kicked and punched his way through the yelling throng.

Then Eglofstein appeared, and I saw the colonel turn on him

in a fury. The adjutant recoiled as if he had been struck and shrugged his shoulders. A moment later they were hidden from view by a phalanx of dim, silent figures: Donop was leading his company in double-quick time to the Sanroque outwork, where fighting seemed to be in progress. Borne to my ears on the wind came the sound of small-arms fire, confused shouting, and a distant flourish of drums.

When Donop's company had gone by, I again caught sight of the colonel. He was standing outside the convent door giving orders to two grenadiers, who, equipped with pickaxes and wet cloths, were about to break into the burning building. As I watched the colonel standing there with folded arms, I was transfixed by a sudden pang of horror: my sabre, double-barrelled pistol and leather gloves must still be in the chapel, somewhere on the flagstones beside the table, together with those of Eglofstein, Donop and Brockendorf! My heart missed a beat, and everything within me cried: "Jesus Mary, those grenadiers will find them! We're done for. Now it cannot fail to come out that the signal was given by us, not the Marquis of Bolibar!"

But the two men returned, reeling and half-senseless, their beards singed and their clothes, faces and hands black with soot. One of them had his arm swathed in bloody rags where a shell splinter had pierced his wrist. They had ventured no more than a hundred paces into the convent before turning back. By the grace of God, to whom I secretly gave thanks for his assistance, every room and passage in the building was filled with a dense pall of smoke.

The colonel and Eglofstein vaulted into the saddle, and, braving the wind-fanned flames that had already engulfed the Calle Geronimo, galloped off down the street toward Santa Engracia Hospital, for word had come that this building, too, was menaced by fire.

The rest had also dispersed, so the street was now deserted. Brockendorf and I had remained behind with my corporal, Thiele, and another eight or nine of my men who were either unafraid or heedless of the danger that threatened them. Fed by the quantities of tow and oaten straw stored on the ground floor of the convent, the fire might at any moment ignite the powder kegs arrayed in the refectory, chapter house and passages. Being powerless to avert this disaster, we confined ourselves to preventing the flames from spreading to the houses round about.

Brockendorf called to me to withdraw to the other end of the street and cordon it off so that no one could approach the convent, for some loud detonations from inside the building – two in quick succession – told us that a brace of powder kegs had already gone up.

The wind howled, driving fat flakes of wet snow into my face. The street was bright as daylight, and the windows of the blazing convent glowed as though lit by the setting sun.

The guns were still thundering away at the town, but the fire near the town hall seemed to be under control at last.

I suddenly saw, as I was standing at my post, a band of horsemen galloping straight for the cordon with a clatter of hoofs, Salignac at their head.

He wore neither helmet nor cloak, but he carried a naked sabre in his hand. His grey moustache was bedraggled and his pale face convulsed with excitement. I stepped forward and barred his path.

"Your pardon, Captain, but you cannot pass."

"Out of my way," he cried, reining in just short of me.

"This street is closed. I cannot guarantee your safety."

"My safety? What business of yours is that? Look to your own. Stand aside, I say."

He spurred his charger on and brandished his sabre above my head.

"I have my orders," I shouted, "and they are –"

"To hell with your orders! Make way!"

I stood aside, and he galloped past me with his men following on behind. Once outside the convent he dismounted. His tunic and boots were plastered all over with mud as if a cannon ball had missed him by inches. He gazed around him with a wild and ferocious air.

Brockendorf came panting up from the other end of the street.

"Salignac!" he called as he came. "What in the world do you want?"

"Is he still here? Have you seen him?"

"Whom do you seek? The colonel?"

"I seek the Marquis of Bolibar!" cried Salignac, and never before had I heard such hatred and contempt in a human voice.

"The Marquis of Bolibar?" Brockendorf repeated helplessly, staring at Salignac open-mouthed.

"Is he gone? Has he escaped?"

"I cannot say," Brockendorf blurted out, utterly bemused. "He hasn't left by this door."

"So he must still be in there," Salignac exclaimed with the relish of Satan gloating over a lost soul. "He won't escape me this time." He turned to his dragoons. "We have him at last, the traitor. Dismount and follow me."

The dragoons were uneasy, I could tell. They shook their heads and glanced irresolutely, first at their commanding officer, then at the blazing convent.

"Salignac!" Brockendorf protested, aghast at the captain's lunatic scheme. "You're going to your death. The powder! Nothing can prevent it from –"

Salignac ignored him. "Forward!" he cried. "Any man of you worth his salt, come with me!"

Four of the dragoons, dauntless and intrepid veterans of a hundred engagements since Marengo, leapt off their horses.

"Comrades," said one of them, "there's only one heaven for the brave, and that's where we'll meet again."

"You're insane!" Brockendorf bellowed.

"Long live the Emperor!" cried Salignac, brandishing his sabre. "Long live the Emperor!" echoed the dragoons, and we saw all five men dash through the doorway into a tornado of glowing ashes.

We stood there, mute and motionless.

"He'll turn back when he sees how it is," Brockendorf said after a while.

"He'll never turn back," came Corporal Thiele's voice from behind me. "Not he, Captain."

125

"Not a mortal soul will ever leave that hell alive," exclaimed someone else.

Thiele nodded. "No, not a mortal soul."

"He's pursuing a phantom to his death," I whispered to Brockendorf, "and we're to blame."

"I should have told him the truth," groaned Brockendorf. "I should have told him, God forgive me."

"Salignac!" I shouted into the inferno, and again: "Salignac!" Too late. No answer.

"That officer," said someone, "– he wanted to die, so it seemed."

"Bravo!" cried Corporal Thiele. "You've guessed it, my lad. I know him of old – I know he goes looking for death." He paused. "God in heaven, what's that?"

We were suddenly shrouded in darkness. A terrible cloud of smoke filled the street, to be dispersed a moment later by the wind. Then came a violent explosion that hurled me to the ground. The horses shied and raced off down the street with their riders. Silence ensued – a long, deathly hush that endured until I heard Brockendorf yelling like a madman.

"Get away from here! Back! It's the powder!"

I found myself in the doorway of the house across the street, not knowing how I had got there so quickly. From overhead came a mighty whistling and roaring, hissing and whirring. Stones and balks of timber, gobbets of fire and fragments of blazing wood spun through the air and pattered down like hailstones. The convent wall had burst asunder to reveal a sea of flames so frightful that the very sight made me tremble.

Corporal Thiele dashed across the street, arms flailing, and flung himself down in a breathless heap beside me. I could everywhere see men cowering against walls and shielding their faces from the wind-blown smoke and red-hot ash. A corpse lay sprawled beneath a blazing beam in the middle of the street.

"Jochberg!" It was Brockendorf's voice, but I could neither see him nor make out where he had taken refuge. "Jochberg, where are you? Are you still alive?"

"Here I am, over here!" I shouted. "And you? And Salignac? Where is he? Can you see him?"

"Dead!" Brockendorf called back. "No one could escape that inferno."

"Salignac!" I cried above the hellish din, and for a while we all listened, though without hope.

"Salignac!" I called again. "Salignac!"

"Who calls? Here I am," came a voice, and all at once Salignac emerged from the smoke and flames. His clothes were smouldering, the bandage around his head was charred, and the blade of his sabre, which he still held aloft, was red-hot to the hilt. But there he stood before my unbelieving eyes – there he stood, spewed out alive by that holocaust of death and destruction.

I stared at him, at a loss for words, but Brockendorf gave a jubilant exclamation.

"Why, Salignac, you're alive!" he cried, his voice betraying a mixture of joy and amazement, disbelief and dread. "We'd given you up for lost."

The cavalry captain threw back his head and laughed – a gruesome sound that rings in my ears to this day.

"Where are the others?" called Brockendorf, but Salignac ignored the question.

"If the Marquis of Bolibar was in there, he'll give no third signal."

Just then a rafter broke away from the roof, somersaulted through the air, and landed with a crash at Salignac's feet.

"Over here, Salignac!" I heard Brockendorf shout, and then his voice was drowned by a mighty roar.

Salignac continued to stand there, erect and unmoving, as the convent's shattered wall caved in and collapsed with a sound like thunder. Flames shot into the air and blazing debris showered the roadway, but I saw him deliberately set off down the street amid those swirling, darting tongues of fire, those hurtling timbers and blocks of stone, as if exempt from the death and destruction around him.

A PRAYER

Lieutenant Lohwasser of the Hessian Regiment, who came to relieve us with his platoon at two in the morning, was the first to bring word that the insurgents had taken advantage of the confusion occasioned by the fire to drive our men back and capture the Sanroque, Estrella and Mon Cœur outworks. The Hessians, reinforced by Günther's and Donop's companies, were holding our last fortified line, which intersected with the river Alcar a stone's throw from the walls of the town.

The bombardment had by then diminished in intensity, and only an occasional shot rang out to deter any of the townsfolk who had ventured forth and shoo them back into their subterranean burrows. Even this sporadic musket fire ceased as the night wore on, perhaps because the attackers had attained their first objective and were now awaiting fresh orders from the Marquis of Bolibar.

Just as the relief detachment arrived, the town was engulfed by a violent storm that began with driving snow and ended in torrential rain. The narrow lanes were flooded and the ground turned soft within minutes. I waded along, ankle-deep in mire, shivering with cold and soaked to the skin. Back in my billet I threw myself down on the bed fully clothed and slept for three hours, but toward five in the morning I was roused by one of the colonel's orderlies and summoned to headquarters without delay.

It was still pitch dark when I left my billet. The atmosphere was humid and the sky heavily overcast. I shivered, less with cold than with the vague unease and misgiving that had taken hold of me, for I naturally assumed that the truth was out, and that the colonel wished to see me because I had been present when Donop and Brockendorf gave the organ signal in the night.

I walked with slow and irresolute tread, pausing and making detours in the hope of delaying my interview with the colonel until I had conferred with Brockendorf and Donop, but neither of them was in his quarters. Their doors were locked and their windows in darkness, nor did I encounter them on the way. The only figures that loomed up out of the murk were those of Spaniards bearing lanterns; now, after all the terrors of the night, men and women from every part of the town were streaming toward the church of Nuestra Señora del Pilar to draw comfort and reassurance from the words of the Mass.

On reaching the orderly-room, which I entered with a pounding heart, I found it occupied by such officers of the Nassau and Hessian Regiments as were not on duty or manning the fortifications. In their midst I saw Salignac wearing the half nonchalant, half peevish expression typical of seasoned officers of the Emperor's old guard when denied an opportunity to risk their lives in battle. He threw me a glance from beneath his shaggy grey eyebrows as I walked in – a piercing, hostile glance from which I seemed to infer that, although he well remembered our last night's meeting, I would do better not to mention it.

Günther, whose shoulder had been pierced by a musket ball, was lying on a camp-bed in the room next door, groaning and delirious. He had been brought there because the hospital was overflowing with sick and wounded, and the surgeon of the Hessian Regiment was standing at his bedside, tearing a woman's tattered old shift into strips in readiness to renew his dressing.

Close on my heels came Captain Count Schenk zu Castel-Borckenstein of the Hessians, accompanied by his greyhound. He was limping and leaning on a stick, having injured his left leg during the precipitate retreat from the Mon Cœur lunette. Promptly addressing himself to Eglofstein in an irate and petulant tone, he demanded to know why he had been summoned. He had come straight from the outer defences, he said, and his presence was surely more needful there than here. Eglofstein shrugged and silently indicated the colonel, who was perched on the edge of the adjutant's desk. Brockendorf, too, proceeded to grumble. His men had still to be allotted billets and were knee-deep in the mire of the streets, he complained. They were soaked to the skin.

The colonel looked up, spread a map of the town and its environs across his knees, and called for silence.

I heard a whispering around me when he began to speak, and fancied for a moment that all eyes had turned in my direction – that I was on trial, and that the others had gathered to pass judgement on me. Donop, too, stared glumly at the floor and Eglofstein stole anxious glances at the bed on which Günther lay wounded. Brockendorf alone looked defiant, his sullen and impatient demeanour conveying that he had already wasted too much time on the business in hand.

The colonel's first few words sufficed to show me how groundless my fears had been, however, for it soon became clear that he had not discovered the truth, and that he still considered the Marquis of Bolibar to be the traitor in our midst.

My dire forebodings melted away, and the suspense that had kept me on my feet relaxed its grip. Perceiving only now how weary I was, I sank down on a heap of firewood beside the stove.

The colonel, whose talk was all of the night's hostilities, commended the fortitude of the Hessian troops and the sangfroid displayed by their officers. Of our own regiment he made no mention at all. The Hessian officers regarded us with supercilious smiles, much to Donop's annoyance.

"If only they had all stood fast like Günther," he murmured to Captain Eglofstein, "the outworks would still be ours."

Lieutenant von Dubitsch of the Crown Prince's Own, a corpulent man as ruddy-cheeked as a cook who spends his days boiling crabs, overheard Donop's gibe and turned on him.

"What was that? Are you suggesting that one of us failed in his duty?"

"You heard what the colonel said," Captain Castel-Borckenstein thundered. "My grenadiers were the last to withdraw from the redoubt."

130

Donop made no reply, but he put his lips close to Eglofstein's ear and whispered just loud enough for the others to hear.

"I came in time to see them take to their heels. They were in such a hurry, they bounded along like March hares."

This provoked a general altercation. Barbed remarks flew back and forth. Lieutenant von Dubitsch bellowed at Donop with cheeks empurpled, feet stamped, spurs jingled, Castel-Borckenstein's greyhound barked. At last the colonel smote the table with his fist and bade the warring parties be silent.

The tumult subsided and the antagonists regarded each other with mute ill-will and contempt. Brockendorf alone refused to be quelled. He had taken advantage of the general hubbub to vent his own displeasure, complaining that his company's quarters had been burned down, and that they had yet to be allotted others.

"For how much longer," he cried, "must my men bivouack outside in the rain? Are they to wait till the mire closes over their heads?"

"I assigned your men fresh quarters an hour ago," the colonel told him curtly.

"Quarters? Is that what you call them? A sheepcote and a barn sufficient to house but a quarter of their number, and swarming with rats into the bargain!"

"There's room enough for two companies, Brockendorf. Why must you always carp and cavil?"

"Colonel, it's my duty to –"

"Your duty is to hold your tongue and obey my orders, is that clear?"

"I'm obliged to you, Colonel," snarled Brockendorf, sweating with rage. "The rank and file can drown in mud provided every gentleman on the staff has his own well-heated room and –"

He swallowed the rest of what he had meant to say, for the colonel had sprung to his feet and confronted him. His cheeks were suffused, his fists clenched, the veins in his forehead swollen.

"Captain," he roared, "you seem to find your sword a

burden. Should you wish to surrender it, the guard-room isn't far."

Brockendorf retreated a step. He stared at the colonel, then bowed his head and fell silent. Courage and defiance deserted him whenever our commanding officer lost his temper. The colonel slowly turned about and resumed his seat.

Silence reigned for a full minute. No one stirred and nothing could be heard save the crackle of the stove and the rustle of the papers in the colonel's hands. Then he calmly continued his exposition in a voice that gave no hint of what had gone before.

"This town and its garrison are in dire straits," he said, "although the insurgents are unlikely to renew their assault in the immediate future. I have it on good authority" – here he briefly paused and glanced at Captain de Salignac – "that the Marquis of Bolibar, who directed the enemy's operations by means of signals given from within the town, was killed when our powder magazine exploded. For the present, therefore, the insurgents are leaderless and disorganized. All depends on whether d'Hilliers' brigade reaches here before the guerrillas learn that their clandestine commander and strategist is dead. If they renew their attack we're lost, for the plain truth is" – the colonel drew a deep breath and hesitated – "we have no powder left."

"Water!" came a shrill cry from the inner room where Günther lay. The surgeon, who had been leaning in the doorway pipe in hand, listening to the colonel's account of our predicament, took a pitcher of water and hurried to the wounded man's bedside.

"No powder left?" Lieutenant von Dubitsch repeated in a halting voice. Eglofstein nodded gravely. We stood there, helpless and utterly dismayed, for none of us had suspected that the position was so desperate.

"It is, therefore, of paramount importance," the colonel resumed, "that General d'Hilliers should be apprised of the garrison's plight. Here is my letter to him. I have summoned you here because one of you must undertake to carry it through the guerrillas' lines."

A brooding silence descended on the room. Salignac alone came to attention, stepped forward, and halted as though awaiting orders.

"You ask the impossible," Castel-Borckenstein said softly.

"I do not," the colonel exclaimed. "All that's needed is a man with the requisite courage and cunning – a man who speaks Spanish and will disguise himself as a peasant or muleteer."

Salignac faced about and returned to his corner without a word.

"A man who'll be hanged if he falls into the guerrillas' hands," said First-Lieutenant von Froben of the Hessians. He laughed mirthlessly and drew a hand over his perspiring brow.

"That's true," Lieutenant von Dubitsch chimed in, breathless with agitation. "While inspecting our outposts this morning I was hailed by a voice from the enemy lines. Did I know that last year's harvest of hemp was abundant, it asked, and that rope enough to hang us all would cost but little?"

"Quite so," the colonel said calmly. "The insurgents hang their prisoners – that's stale news – but an attempt must be made nonetheless. Whichever of you volunteers for this dangerous mission may rest assured that –"

We all flinched, startled by a strident peal of laughter, and turned to see that Günther's fever had driven him from his bed. He was standing on the threshold, cackling, with one hand gripping the door-post and the other the hem of his red woollen blanket. He did not see us. His darting eyes seemed intent on something far away, and his delirious condition led him to fancy that he was at home with his father and mother, having just arrived with the mail coach from Spain. He dropped the blanket and waved a hand in the air.

"Here I am!" he cried, still laughing. "Are you all asleep in there? Open up, I'm home again. Quickly, to work! Slaughter me a pig, kill me a goose, send for wine and music! *Allegro, allegro!*"

The surgeon caught him by the arm and tried to coax him back to bed, but Günther recognized the man despite his fever and thrust him away.

"Leave me be, surgeon. All you can do is wield a razor and open a vein, and neither to much effect."

The surgeon dropped his pipe, he was so taken aback. He glanced at the colonel in some confusion and sprang to his own and Günther's defence.

"That's the fever talking," he said, "– anyone can tell."

"I'm not so sure," said the colonel, clearly annoyed by the interruption. "Get him out of here."

"I'm a sick man, truly I am," Günther sighed, gazing at some distant prospect above our heads. "It's bad for the liver to wash a hot meal down with cold beer, the verger's wife told me so."

"He'll not live to see his mother's cat again," Dubitsch murmured to Castel-Borckenstein.

Meantime, the surgeon had contrived to shepherd his delirious patient back to bed. He was a thoroughly skilful practitioner, albeit none of us gave him the credit he deserved, and had some years earlier written a short treatise on the essential nature of melancholy.

The colonel settled himself again, glanced at his watch, and readdressed himself to his officers.

"Time presses. Any further delay could spell disaster. To repeat: whichever of you volunteers for this mission may rest assured that I shall bring him to the Emperor's notice. He may also count on immediate promotion."

The silence was so complete that I could hear Günther breathing in the room next door. Brockendorf looked irresolute, Donop shook his head, Castel-Borckenstein sheepishly pointed to his injured leg, and Dubitsch tried to interpose Brockendorf's broad back between himself and the colonel's gaze.

There was a sudden movement at the back of the room. Someone pushed past Dubitsch and Brockendorf, thrust Eglofstein aside, and strode up to the colonel. It was Salignac.

"Let me go, Colonel," he said quickly, glancing around for fear another might forestall him. His sallow face glowed with eagerness for the fray and the Légion d'Honneur on his chest caught the candlelight. Watching him as he stood there a trifle crouched with his hands grasping invisible reins, I seemed to see him already in the saddle and galloping hell-for-leather through the rebel lines.

The colonel gave him a long look, then shook his hand.

"You're a brave man, Salignac. I thank you and shall report your conduct to the Emperor. Return to your billet at once and put on whatever disguise you think best. Lieutenant Jochberg will escort you as far as the enemy lines. I shall expect you back here a quarter of an hour from now, ready to receive your orders. The rest of you may dismiss."

The orderly-room began to empty. Lieutenant von Dubitsch, relieved that someone else had undertaken such a dangerous mission, was the first to go. Eglofstein and Castel-Borckenstein lingered at the door for a moment, each determined to give the other precedence.

Castel-Borckenstein made an infinitesimal gesture of invitation. "Baron?" he said.

"Count?" Eglofstein rejoined with a stiff little bow.

Someone blew out the candles. I continued to hug the stove in the darkness, loath to leave the warmth that was drying my sodden clothes. The colonel's gruff, indignant voice made itself heard outside.

"Well, Brockendorf, what the devil do you want now?"

"It's about our quarters, Colonel," Brockendorf said pleadingly.

"Brockendorf, you're pestering me again. I already told you: there *are* no other quarters."

"But Colonel, I know of a billet that would house my whole company."

"Very well, take it. Why trouble me if you know of one?"

Brockendorf hesitated. "The Spaniards, Colonel . . ."

"The Spaniards? Pay no heed to the Spaniards – throw them out. Let them fend for themselves."

"Bravo, Colonel, no sooner said than done!" Brockendorf cried delightedly. I heard him blunder down the short flight of steps to the street, loudly voicing his heartfelt enthusiasm as he went.

"A paragon, our colonel!" he exclaimed. "A true father to

his men, I've always said so. Anyone who maligns him is a blackguard!"

The colonel's ponderous footsteps receded into the interior of the house. A door closed and silence fell, broken only by the crackle of the flames in the stove.

I saw, when my eyes had become accustomed to the darkness around me, that I was not alone: Salignac was still standing in the middle of the room.

Years have gone by since then. Looking back, I find that the passage of time has cast an uncertain twilight over much that once stood out sharp and distinct in my mind's eye, and I sometimes fancy that Salignac's strange conversation with someone invisible to me was merely a dream. But no, I was awake, I know. It was only when Eglofstein returned with the colonel and the room was illumined by their candle's friendly light – only in that brief instant that I yielded to the illusion that their entrance had roused me from a sinister and oppressive nightmare. An illusion it was, however. I was awake throughout, and I clearly recall my surprise on discerning Salignac's figure in the gloom. I wondered why he had remained behind, for I knew that he had been ordered to return to his quarters and disguise himself as a Spanish peasant or muleteer. Time went by, but still he continued to stand motionless, staring at the wall.

I naturally concluded, when I heard him whispering, that there must be someone else in the room – Donop, perhaps, or one of the Hessian officers, or the surgeon, but what could they be discussing in the darkness with such secrecy? My eyes explored the gloom. The desk, the chair with Eglofstein's cloak draped over the arm, the two oak chests containing regimental papers, the small table in the corner on which lay Eglofstein's silver field toilet and an earthenware wash-basin – all these things I made out, together with Salignac's shadowy form in the middle of the room, but of the surgeon or some brother officer I could see no sign.

Weary though I was, the spectacle aroused my curiosity. With whom could Salignac be conversing so earnestly, and where could that mysterious, unseen personage be lurking? I closed my eyes the better to listen, but Salignac's low voice was drowned by the wind that rattled the door and buffeted the windows. The warmth of the stove, which bathed part of the room in a faint glow, was making me drowsy. I groped my way back to the heap of firewood and pillowed my head on my arms, and it may be that I truly dozed off for some moments before Salignac's laughter jolted me awake.

Salignac was laughing, yes, but not in any mirthful way. His laughter conveyed some indefinable emotion. Hatred, perhaps, or defiance and disdain? No, none of those. Despair and dread? Not those either. Derision and contempt? No, I had never before heard such laughter and could fathom its significance as little as I understood the words its author flung at empty space a moment later.

"Do you call me again?" I heard him cry. "Ah no, Kindly One, from you I hope for nothing. Ah no, Wise and Merciful One, you have too often betrayed me in the past."

I pressed close to the wall and listened with bated breath as Salignac went on.

"You mean to delude me with false hopes – you mean to see me disappointed, afflicted and despairing. I know your cruel purpose. No, Righteous One, you that beguile time and eternity with your vengeful whims, I mistrust you. I know that you never forget."

He fell silent as if listening to some voice that came to him out of the roar of the wind and the rain. Then, slowly and reluctantly, he took a step forward.

"You order me? Very well, I must obey you still. Is that your wish? So be it, I shall go, but know this: the journey on which you send me I undertake for one who is mightier than you."

Again he listened unspeaking in the gloom, and again I could not tell whence – from what abyss or far-off place – his answer came, for I heard none of it. He drew himself erect.

"Your voice is as the tempest, yet I do not flinch. He whom I serve has the mouth of a lion, and his voice rings out across the blood-stained fields of this world from a thousand throats."

All at once the fire in the stove flared up and gave me a momentary glimpse of his sallow, ecstatic face. Then darkness enveloped it once more.

"Yes," I heard him exult, "it is he! Do not lie! He is the Promised One, the Just One, for all the exalted signs are fulfilled. He is come from the island of the sea and wears ten crowns upon his head, as it was foretold. Where is his equal, and who can contend with him? Power has been given him over all nations, and all who dwell on earth shall worship him!"

I shrank when I heard these words, because I recognized them as a description of the Antichrist, the foe of mankind who employs his portents and marvels, victories and triumphs to exalt himself above God and His servants. The seals of life were shattered before my eyes, and I suddenly discerned the ferment of the age and perceived its mysterious, terrible purpose. Overcome with horror, I yearned to jump up, flee from the room and be alone, but my limbs would not move. I lay there like a helpless captive whose chest is crushed by some mountainous weight, and the voice in the darkness, gaining strength, rang out in triumph and rebellion, exultation and defiance.

"Tremble, wretch that you are! The end of your power is nigh. Where are those that fight on your behalf? Where are the hundred and forty-four thousand who wear your name upon their brow? Them I cannot see, but He is come, the Terrible One, the Vanquisher, and He will destroy your earthly kingdom!"

I strove to cry out, but in vain. All that escaped my lips was a low, agonized groan, and I was again compelled to hear the voice that rose above the roar of the wind and the rain, which continued to buffet the window-panes without respite.

"I stand here before you, as I did of old, and see you as powerless and dispirited as you were then. What is there to prevent me from raising my fist once more and driving it into that hateful countenance?"

He broke off abruptly as the door swung open and candlelight flooded the room. Eglofstein and the colonel appeared on the threshold.

138

For a fraction of a second I saw Salignac gazing, fist clenched and face contorted, at an effigy of the Redeemer mounted on the whitewashed wall. Then his rigid features relaxed. He lowered his arm, turned about, and calmly walked over to the colonel, who stared at him and frowned.

"Still here, Salignac? I ordered you to return to your quarters and make ready. Time is running out. What have you been doing?"

"Praying, Colonel," said Salignac, "but I'm ready now."

The colonel had meanwhile looked around the room and caught sight of me.

"Why, there's Jochberg," he said with a smile. "The youngster fell asleep beside the stove, I'll warrant. Well, Jochberg, you look as if you're fresh from the arms of Morpheus."

Although I myself felt as if I had slept and dreamed heavily, I shook my head. The colonel paid me no further attention and readdressed himself to Salignac.

"You were instructed to take off your uniform and disguise yourself as a peasant or muleteer."

"I propose to ride as I am, Colonel."

The colonel's expression was a mixture of surprise, anger and dismay.

"Are you mad, Salignac?" he said sharply. "You'll be shot by the first enemy sentry to set eyes on you."

"I'll ride him down."

"The bridge over the Alcar is within range of the enemy's guns."

"I'll cross it at a gallop."

The colonel stamped his foot in a rage.

"Damned obstinacy! Figueras lies on your route, and the guerrillas hold the village in strength. You'll never get through."

Salignac drew himself up proudly.

"Would you teach me how to wield my sabre, Colonel?"

"Be reasonable, Salignac!" cried the colonel, thoroughly at a loss now. "The fate of the regiment – indeed, the success of the whole campaign – depends on the outcome of your mission."

"You may rest easy on that score, Colonel," Salignac replied with perfect equanimity.

The colonel paced furiously up and down the room. Then Eglofstein stepped in.

"I've known the captain since the East Prussian campaign," he said. "If anyone can get through the guerrillas' lines unscathed – by God, he's the man."

The colonel stood there irresolutely for a while, thinking hard. Then he shrugged.

"Very well," he grunted. "How you get through is your business, after all, no one else's." He took the map from the table, unfolded it, and pointed out the spot where Salignac was to meet General d'Hilliers' advance guard.

"I'll lend you my best horse, the dun that bears the brand of the Ivenec stud. Ride like the wind."

We passed Günther's room on the way out. The fever seemed to have left him for a space, and he was half sitting up in bed.

"How goes it, Günther?" the colonel asked him in passing.

"I'm wounded *mortaliter*," he mumbled, "– *bestialiter, diaboliter*." Then his mind clouded over again. "Donop!" he called. "Can you understand my Latin? Don't weep, dearest, I told you not to. You look like Mary Magdalene when you weep . . ."

We opened the door and went out. The first rays of a dismal dawn were visible in the east. The colonel shook Salignac by the hand.

"It's time. Do your best, but have a care. May God preserve you."

"Never fear, Colonel," Salignac said serenely, "– he will."

140

THE COURIER

The sun had not yet risen when we left our lines toward seven that morning, and all that could be seen in the sky was the moon, which floated among the louring clouds like a big silver thaler. Corporal Thiele and four dragoons came with us. We were all unmounted save Salignac, who was leading his horse by the bridle. The dun proceeded at a placid walk, head bowed.

We came upon our outermost line of sentries where the buckthorn bushes began. A sergeant and two grenadiers were stretched out on the ground, their greatcoats beaded with moisture and their shakos filmed with rime. The sergeant rose as we approached and kicked aside the pack of cards with which he and his comrades intended to play as soon as it became light enough. He did not trouble to ask for the password because he knew me and Corporal Thiele by sight.

"Colonel's courier on a special mission," Salignac told him curtly. The sergeant raised a hand to his cap in salute before resuming his seat on the ground. He rubbed his hands, shivering, and complained that he did not know how he would get the muskets to fire after a whole night of rain.

"There'll be more rain today," he said, "– warm rain. The toads and snails are venturing out of their holes."

Being tired and hungry, none of us felt disposed to engage in a conversation about the weather. We walked on. Our route took us straight through the scrub for a stretch; then we bore left. The dun, scenting the proximity of water, pricked up its ears and snorted softly.

The eastern sky paled, the wind drove swaths of mist across

hill and meadow. Ahead of us, half devoured by foxes and birds of prey, lay a dead horse with a gaping wound in its flank. A flock of crows took wing as we approached and disappeared in the direction of the Alcar, cawing harshly. One lone bird, which turned back half-way and fluttered above us in great agitation, refused to be driven off.

Thiele paused and shook his head.

"Carrion crows are birds of ill omen," he growled. "Look at Satan's ambassador there. Now we know that one of us will stop a bullet this morning."

"That's not hard to predict," retorted one of the dragoons, glancing at Salignac, "and I know who he is, with or without the help of that Devil's messenger."

"It's a shame," said another, "– a shame to see a gallant officer go to his death in vain."

Thiele shook his head.

"Not he," he said. "He's not going to his death. You don't know him."

For a while we followed the course of the Alcar. The wind sang in the reeds that clothed its banks. On the other side we could see the long line of watchfires around which the guerrillas had spent the night. Then we changed direction and started up a hill overgrown with cork oaks. At its summit I saw a hut of the kind in which vine-dressers customarily kept their implements.

Just as I turned my back on the river, however, I was struck by a sudden thought and hurried in Salignac's wake.

I caught him up. His horse, which had slipped on the muddy ground, was lashing out and trying to bite. To calm the beast, Salignac offered it some morsels of bread from his pocket.

"It occurs to me," I said as I panted along beside him, "that if someone rowed upstream, keeping to the lee of the trees on the bank, he would very likely be out of range by the time the guerrillas sighted him."

"Jochberg," said Salignac without looking round, and his tone implied that I was frightened for myself, not for him, "take your men and go back. I have no more need of your assistance."

"Whether or not you need me," I replied, "my orders are to

escort you to the enemy lines. We have little farther to go in any case, as you can see."

It was light by now. Hidden from view by the cork oaks' massive trunks, we had approached to within a hundred paces of the hut. A thin column of blackish smoke was rising from behind the stakes of the fence that enclosed it. We were, beyond doubt, confronted by a rebel outpost whose occupants had lit a fire on which to boil soup or roast maize cobs.

We paused among some thorn-apple and buckthorn bushes and waited for Thiele and his men to come up with us. Then we held a whispered conference on how best to take the hut. We all agreed that the insurgents must not be given time to fire a shot, for that would have brought the enemy down on us in hundreds.

We made ready. One of the dragoons took a swig of brandy and offered me his canteen. Then I gave the signal and we charged silently up the hill.

We were almost at the top when we saw the guerrillas' coloured stocking-caps and their startled, dismayed faces appear above the fence, but Corporal Thiele and I were already vaulting over it. One of our adversaries drew a bead on Thiele, but I dashed the carbine from his hands as I landed on the other side. Then the rest of my men swarmed over the fence, and the guerrillas, finding themselves at a disadvantage, surrendered with a curse or two but little active resistance. There were three of them. They wore jackets of brown cloth and, over these, sashes whose ends were woven with silver thread. Just then a fourth rebel emerged from the hut with a cauldron in his hand, having evidently been about to go down to the river to fetch water.

He was a giant of a man, a Carmelite friar with a sword belted about his habit. He dropped the cauldron when he saw us. Instead of drawing his sword, however, he stooped to pick up an axle-tree and, whirling this lethal weapon above his head, set about us.

We had some difficulty in disarming him, being unable to open fire. Thiele sustained a blow that numbed his arm for several minutes, but we at last contrived to wrest the axle-tree

143

from the friar's grasp. Then we shut the guerrillas in the hut, all four of them, and barred the door.

Our task was complete. The dragoons found some slices of raw mule flesh and spitted them on their sabres to roast over the fire. Thiele's tobacco-pipe went the rounds. Meanwhile, Salignac strode impatiently up and down. At length, after pausing to adjust his horse's girth and stirrup, he came over to me.

"It's time, Jochberg. Give me the letter."

I handed him the pouch containing the map, a compass, and the dispatch addressed to General d'Hilliers. Followed by the rest of us, he led his horse out of the enclosure.

Our present position commanded an excellent view of the hilly terrain around us. Visible on every side were detachments of guerrillas large and small, many mounted with others on foot. Sentries paced the entrenchments with muskets shouldered, pack-mules congested the crossroads, a supply waggon drawn by oxen lumbered slowly over the bridge, horses were led to water, a distant trumpet summoned troops to muster, and two officers, recognizable as such by their thick pigtails and three-cornered hats, emerged from the door of the farmhouse.

Salignac had already mounted up. The dragoons eyed him with covert concern, and every man of us shuddered at the reckless impossibility of the venture. He bent forward in the saddle and gave the dun two lumps of sugar steeped in port wine. Then, with a perfunctory wave to me, he spurred his horse into motion. There was a jingle of harness, and a moment later he was careering down the hill.

I did my best to seem calm, but my hands were trembling with excitement. The lips of the man beside me shaped a silent prayer.

A shot rang out quite close at hand. We all flinched as if we had never heard a musket fired before, but Salignac rode on with scarcely a turn of the head, a white plume of snow streaming out behind him.

He vanished into a small copse of chestnut trees, only to reappear within seconds.

Another shot rang out, and another, and a third. Salignac sat his saddle like a rock. A man darted out from behind a hedge and tried to seize his reins. He drew back his arm, felled him with a sabre-stroke, and sped straight on like a steeplechaser. He looked neither right nor left, seemingly blind to what was going on around him.

By now the entire countryside was in turmoil. Guerrillas were clambering out of their trenches and horsemen converging on Salignac from all sides, yelling as they galloped at full stretch. A crisp rattle of musketry made itself heard, and puffs of blue powder-smoke rose into the air. Salignac rode straight through the tumult, standing in his stirrups and brandishing his sabre. He was almost at the bridge. Then I saw them, by heaven: there were men on the bridge, six or eight of them – no nine! No, ten or more! Couldn't he see them? He was on top of them now. One of them levelled a musket, Salignac's charger reared – he was done for! But no, he soared over their heads and across the bridge, leaving two of them sprawled in the roadway.

It was a spectacle so awesome, so heart-stopping, that I forgot to breathe. Only when the immediate danger was past did I become aware that I had seized Thiele's hand in my excitement and was gripping it convulsively. I let go of it. Salignac was now on the farther bank, whose wooded slopes gave promise of safety, but a moment later – someone beside me cried out in alarm – a band of horsemen burst from the trees and cut the courier off. Was he blind? "Veer left!" I shouted, though I knew he could not hear me. "Veer left!" Then they were on him. His horse fell and I could see him no longer, merely a confusion of heads, horses' manes, whirling blades, musket barrels, upraised arms – a surging, rearing, plunging mass of struggling human forms. Nothing could save Salignac now: his ride was at an end.

I heard a faint whistle, a sound familiar to me from a score of engagements, and ducked. Thiele, who was standing in front of me, sank silently to his knees and toppled over backwards. A stray bullet had found its mark.

"Thiele!" I cried. "Comrade! Are you wounded?"

"I'm done for," the corporal groaned, putting a hand to his chest.

I bent over him and tore his tunic open. Blood was welling from the wound.

I took Thiele by the shoulder, sat him up, and groped for a cloth to serve as a bandage. The others ignored my cries for help. One of them gripped my arm.

"Look, Lieutenant!" he shouted. "Look!"

The mêlée on the farther bank had broken up. Wounded horses were rolling on the ground, men crying quarter and fleeing with their hands in the air. And out of that chaos, still brandishing his sabre, rode Salignac. He was alive and unscathed! Erect in the saddle, he soared over trenches, mounds of snow, men, bushes, earthworks, gabions, shattered gun-carriages, smouldering camp-fires.

I heard laboured breathing beside me and turned to look. Corporal Thiele had propped himself on his hands and was staring after Salignac with glazed eyes.

"Don't you know him now?" he groaned. "I do. That man will never stop a bullet. The four elements have made a pact: fire will not burn him, nor water drown him, nor air desert his lungs, nor earth crush his limbs . . ."

The others' jubilant cries drowned his mutterings. The breath rattled in his throat, and his shirt and tunic were red with blood.

"He's through! He's safe!" the dragoons shouted exultantly. They hurled their shakos high in the air, brandished their carbines and.cheered.

"Pray for his sinful soul," were Thiele's last, halting words. "Pray – pray for the Wandering Jew. He cannot die . . ."

INSURRECTION

I had sent one of my dragoons on ahead to bring the colonel immediate word of the course and outcome of Salignac's mission. When I myself entered the orderly-room an hour later, the only person I found there was Captain Castel-Borckenstein, who had come to collect his company's latest orders and was on the point of leaving.

He lingered in the doorway for a moment to ask how matters had gone, and I gave him a brief account of what had happened. I was still speaking when Eglofstein emerged from the adjoining room. Quietly closing the door behind him, he went to the window and beckoned me over.

"I'm at my wits' end," he whispered with an anxious glance at the door. "Nothing will induce him to leave the man's bedside. He clings there like a limpet."

"Whom do you mean?" I asked, puzzled.

"The colonel, of course. Günther is delirious – he has been raving about Françoise-Marie."

Eglofstein's whispered words stabbed me to the heart – rang in my ears like a tocsin. Günther might well betray himself and us in his feverish condition, I could see that danger but had no idea how to avert it. We stared at each other helplessly, both thinking of the colonel's jealousy, his violent temper, his bouts of malicious fury.

"If he learns the truth," said Eglofstein, "God help us and the regiment at large. He'll forget all about the danger of the moment, our desperate predicament, the guerrillas, the beleaguered town – he'll forget everything save how to avenge himself on all of us as bloodily as possible."

"Has Günther mentioned her name?"

"No, not yet. He's sleeping now, thank God, but earlier he spoke of her incessantly. He scolded her, he petted her, he chided and cajoled her, and the colonel stood there waiting for him to say her name as eagerly as Satan gloating over a lost soul." Eglofstein caught me by the arm. "Where are you going, Jochberg? Stay here, you'll wake him!"

Heedless of Eglofstein's warning, I tiptoed into Lieutenant von Günther's sick-room.

Günther was lying in bed, not asleep but muttering and laughing softly to himself. His cheeks were flushed and his eyes as sunken as a pair of empty walnut shells. The surgeon, who was going the rounds of the hospital, had sent one of his assistants, a beardless youth incompetent to do more than refresh the moist cloths on the wounded man's brow.

The colonel was standing at the head of the bed. He looked up as I came in, clearly displeased by my intrusion. I went over to him and reported what he already knew: that his courier had safely crossed the enemy lines an hour before. He listened without taking his eyes off Günther's lips.

"General d'Hilliers will have the letter in his hands in sixteen hours' time," he murmured. "If all goes well we should hear his vanguard's musket-fire three days from now, Jochberg, wouldn't you say? Fourteen leagues, and the roads are built of decent stone."

"Dearest one!" cried Günther, his emaciated hands groping for the woman of his feverish dreams. "Your skin is wonderfully white – white as birch bark . . ."

The colonel's mouth twitched. He bent over Günther and gazed at him as if trying to wrest the name from his lips by main force, yet he already knew full well, as I did, *whose* skin was as white as birch bark.

"Other women," said Günther, chuckling delightedly to himself, "– other women swallow wax, chalk, powdered snail shells and frogs' legs. They smear their faces with a hundred ointments, but to no avail. Their skin is for ever blotched and blistered, poor creatures, whereas yours . . ."

"Go on, go on!" the colonel burst out. I stood there dismayed and despairing, certain that the name would be uttered at any moment. Disaster seemed imminent, but Günther's fever continued to play a mischievous game of cat and mouse with the colonel's jealousy and my fear.

"Be off with you!" he cried, tossing and turning on the bed. "Go away, she doesn't care to see you. What are you doing here, Brockendorf? Your threadbare breeches are as transparent as my sweetheart's lace handkerchief. That comes of sitting too long in taverns, believe me. How's the wine at the 'Pelican' and the 'Blackamoor'? Surgeon? God have mercy on you, Surgeon! What have you done to me?"

His voice became hoarse and the breath issued from his throat in little gasps, and all the while his hands shook with fever.

"Surgeon!" he called again, and groaned aloud. "You'll end on the gibbet some day, mark my words. I can read men's faces like a book."

He sank back exhausted and lay there motionless with his eyes closed, breathing stertorously.

"*Foetida vomit*," said the surgeon's assistant, and dipped a cloth in cold water. "He talks a deal of nonsense."

"Is the end near?" asked the colonel, and I could tell how frantic with fear he was lest Günther should die without uttering his beloved's name.

"*Ultima linea rerum*," the assistant said carelessly as he laid the damp cloth on Günther's brow. "Human aid can avail him little now."

My presence seemed to have slipped the colonel's mind entirely, for he gave every appearance of noticing me again for the first time.

"You may go, Jochberg," he said with a nod. "Leave me alone with him."

I hesitated, reluctant to do as he asked. I was still debating what excuse to give for not budging when I heard footsteps and loud voices in the next room. Then the door opened and Eglofstein came in. Behind him I saw a lanky fellow whom I recognized as a corporal of the Hessian Regiment.

"Softly, softly!" hissed the colonel, indicating the wounded man. "What is it, Eglofstein?"

149

"Colonel, this fellow belongs to Lieutenant Lohwasser's company, which is presently patrolling the streets of the town."

"Yes, yes, I know the man. Well, Corporal, what is it?"

"They're banding together and rioting, sir!" the man announced, all out of breath. "The townsfolk are attacking our sentries and patrols!"

I threw Eglofstein an admiring glance, quite convinced that he had cunningly rehearsed the corporal in this story as a plausible means of weaning the colonel from Günther's bedside, but the colonel merely laughed and shook his head.

"So they've risen in revolt, have they, those pious Christians? Who sent you, Corporal?"

"Lieutenant Lohwasser himself, sir."

"I thought as much." The colonel turned to us and chuckled. "Lohwasser is a scatterbrain – he's for ever imagining things. Tomorrow he'll doubtless report having seen three fiery serpents or Sanctornus the hunchbacked goblin."

At that moment, however, we heard a thunder of footsteps outside. The door was flung open and Lieutenant Donop rushed in.

"Insurrection!" he cried, flushed and breathless from running. "They've attacked our pickets in the marketplace!"

The colonel stopped laughing and turned as white as chalk. The ensuing hush was broken by Günther, now so delirious that he could no longer tell night from day.

"Light the lamp, damn you!" he babbled. "Are you trying to play blind-man's-buff with me, or what?"

"Have the Spaniards gone mad?" the colonel exclaimed. "Fancy attacking our pickets! Hundreds of their countrymen have perished on the gallows for less. What can have possessed them?"

"Brockendorf –" Donop began, then hesitated.

"What of Brockendorf? Where is he?"

"Still in the church."

"In the church? Hell's teeth, is this the moment to hear a sermon? Does he mean to pray for a good wine-harvest while the Spaniards are rioting in the streets?"

150

"Brockendorf and his company have taken up their quarters in the church of Nuestra Señora."

"Quarters . . . in the church!" Purple with rage, the colonel opened and shut his mouth like a stranded fish. He seemed about to choke or fall to the ground in an apoplectic fit.

"I'm dying, God help me," Günther groaned, tossing and turning on the bed. "A thousand good nights, my dearest . . ."

"He says," Donop ventured, "– that's to say, Colonel, Brockendorf claims that you yourself gave the order."

"That *I* gave the order?" fumed the colonel. "So that's it. Now I understand why the Spaniards are in revolt."

He controlled himself with an effort and turned to the corporal.

"You there, double away and fetch me Captain Brockendorf. And you, Donop, summon the priest and the alcalde. Quickly! Why are you still standing there? Eglofstein!"

"Colonel?"

"Those cannon at the crossroads, are they loaded?"

"With case-shot, Colonel. Shall I –"

"Don't open fire unless I order it. Two troops of cavalry will clear the streets."

"With live ammunition?"

"With the butts of their carbines!" the colonel snapped. "I told you: not a shot is to be fired without a direct order from me. Do you want to bring the guerrillas down on our heads?"

"Understood, Colonel."

"Double all pickets. Take ten men, occupy the prefecture and arrest the members of the junta as soon as they assemble. Jochberg?"

"Colonel?"

"Find Captain Castel-Borckenstein. He and his company are to take post in the courtyard behind the guard-house. Not a shot unless I order it, do you understand?"

"Yes, Colonel."

"Then God go with you."

Half a minute later we were all on the way to our appointment with destiny.

★

151

I hurried along the Calle de los Carmelitas with Eglofstein and his men. In the distance, beyond the convent's blackened ruins, we glimpsed the fleeing forms of two Spaniards armed with pitchforks. Our ways parted at the end of the street. Eglofstein was eager to be off, but I, struck by a sudden thought, caught hold of his hands.

"Captain," I said hurriedly, "everything has turned out as the Marquis of Bolibar intended."

"It seems you were right after all, Jochberg," he replied, and made to go.

"Listen," I said. "Günther gave the first signal, that I know for sure. We ourselves – you and I and Brockendorf and Donop – gave the second, and the revolt was provoked by Brockendorf alone. Where, in God's name, is that knife?"

"What knife do you mean, Jochberg?"

"On Christmas Eve, when you had the Marquis shot, you took possession of the knife Saracho gave him – a dagger with an ivory hilt portraying the Virgin and Christ's corpse, don't you remember? It's the last of the three signals. Where did you put that dagger, Captain? I cannot rest while I know you have it."

"The knife," Eglofstein repeated, knitting his brow, "– the dagger . . . Ah yes, the colonel saw me with it and begged it from me for the sake of its fine workmanship. I no longer have it."

My heart leapt at this news.

"All's well, then," I said. "If what you say is true, I'm content. The colonel will never give the third signal, of that I'm certain."

"No indeed, not he," Eglofstein replied with a hollow laugh that failed to disguise his latent guilt and remorse.

On that note we parted and went our separate ways.

THE BLUE BUTTERCUP

I reached Castel-Borckenstein's quarters with ease, for the insurrection was then in its early stages. My return journey was twice as difficult and dangerous, and I soon regretted not having taken a few of Castel-Borckenstein's men with me for protection. Angry rioters were surging through the streets and a hundred furious voices cursing us for a pack of unbelievers whose sole intention was to profane the Christian religion and desecrate its places of worship. Indeed, we were even accused of planning to carry children off to Algiers, there to sell them into slavery. It being customary to paint the Devil in pitch, the priests had spread the blackest lies about us, and the hate-filled mob believed them all, no matter how brazenly false and nonsensical.

Remembering that the colonel had been left alone with Günther, I quickened my pace and, heedless of the pandemonium in the streets, took the shortest way back. I was accosted in the Calle de los Arcades by an old man who warned me to go no further because the end of the street was held by thirty armed Spaniards. This did not alarm me overmuch. In a pinch I could use my pistols to make them see reason, whereas they, whose fire-arms we had confiscated on the morrow of our arrival, had nothing but cudgels, scythes and bread-knives. As I continued on my way, however, a stone whizzed past my head and a woman at a window called out that we were enemies of the Holy Trinity and spurners of the Mother of God, and that Germany was a land inhabited by fire-breathing heretics who merited extinction. Having decided in the end to avoid the main thoroughfare in favour of byways and vegetable gardens, I reached the Calle de los Carmelitas somewhat belated but unscathed.

A half-squadron of dragoons was drawn up outside the colonel's headquarters, awaiting his order to go into action against the insurgents. The priest and the alcalde were just descending the steps under escort, and I learned that they had been instructed to see to it that the rioters laid down their arms and went home within half an hour. On the expiration of that time, any armed civilian encountered in the streets would be summarily shot by the dragoons.

Both men, the priest and the alcalde, looked dismayed and dejected, and seemed far from confident that they would suc-ceed in their mission. Behind them came Brockendorf, the luckless author of the present imbroglio. Since the trio and their escort took up the entire width of the steps, I could not but overhear the heated words that passed between them.

"Our church," the priest exclaimed, "has been ransacked from end to end. All the holy pictures have been stolen."

"That's a lie – a damnable, double-dyed lie!" Brockendorf retorted angrily. "I carried them into the sacristy with my own hands."

"Your men have tethered their horses to the saints' arms," wailed the alcalde. "Horse dung covers the floor knee-deep and the fonts have been converted into mangers. You've made a stable of the house of God!"

Brockendorf blandly ignored this accusation.

"When we hang you," he told the alcalde, "the whole revolt will collapse like a cold syllabub. This town is full of rogues and the gibbets are all untenanted."

The alcalde shot him a venomous glance. I tried to slip past, but Brockendorf caught me by the arm and gestured at the alcalde as if to convey that he was sorry, the matter was out of his hands.

"He must hang," he said. "A pity, for he's a fool of the entertaining sort. He knows an abundance of extremely lewd jests, and I've more than once laughed myself sick at him. Adieu, Jochberg, I'm off to my quarters. The colonel has placed me under arrest."

"Yes, by the grace of God Almighty and Christ and his saints," the priest sighed with wholehearted sincerity.

"Leave Christ and his saints out of this!" cried Brockendorf, stung that the priest should have rendered thanks to God for his punishment. "Words like those sit ill on the lips of a rebel."

I myself upbraided him for having provoked the insurrection, but he rejected my rebuke.

"The sole reason for all this pandemonium," he declared, "is that the Spaniards have taken their quadruples and gold *onzas*, and whatever else they call ducats in this accursed land, and hidden them beneath the flagstones of the church, and now they're afraid I may unearth them. Oh, they're cunning foxes, these Spaniards!"

He released my arm at last, and I ran up the steps. My first glance on entering the orderly-room was directed at the colonel.

He was standing at Günther's bedside, just as I had left him. His face still wore a look of brooding expectancy from which I inferred that our secret had not yet come out. Heedless of the uproar in the streets, he continued to stand listening to the confessions of a man in delirium and striving to interpret his confused hallucinations.

Günther's condition had worsened – indeed, the end seemed imminent – but his lips were still moving. He talked incessantly in short, disjointed snatches while the breath hissed and rattled in his throat. His cheeks and forehead were flushed, his lips parched and cracked. Sometimes muttering, sometimes crying aloud, he was speaking when I entered of some love affair unknown to me.

"If you go to the window and whistle once, the stable-boy will come. You must whistle twice – that will summon the pretty young maidservant . . ."

"What is he saying?" I asked Eglofstein in a low voice.

In lieu of a reply, he took my arm and drew me away from the bed.

"You were gone a long time," he whispered hurriedly. "Now do as I say. Ask no questions, just obey!" Aloud, he went on, "Lieutenant Jochberg, somewhere among our regimental papers I have mislaid an order from the chief of staff relating to the imbursement of arrears of pay. Go through the correspondence of the last few months and read me out each letter and dispatch in order of receipt."

I grasped his intention at once. I was to read aloud to such effect that the colonel would be unable to hear the dying man's tell-tale remarks. Picking up the sheaf of papers which Eglofstein passed across the desk, I began to read.

It was a peculiar situation in which to find myself. As I read, the whole campaign unfolded before my mind's eye, with its trials and tribulations, its battles and hardships, its adventures and dangers, yet the sole purpose of this proceeding was to drown a dying man's last words.

"Order dated 11th September," I declaimed. "*Colonel! It being the desire of His Majesty the Emperor that troops in cantonments be no less well-treated than those in camp, he commands that every man should be daily issued with 16 ounces of meat, 24 ounces of fresh bread, 6 ounces of bread for soup, and* −"

"Those swinish brutes of the Hessian Regiment!" cried Günther, rearing up wildly in his bed. "They sleep together, may heaven forgive them!"

"The next letter," Eglofstein said swiftly. "That was not the one I meant."

"Letter dated 14th December and delivered by Second-Lieutenant Durette of the divisional staff," I went on. "*Marshal Soult desires you, Colonel, to draft a report on the fortress of La Bisbal as soon as you have occupied it. How many cannon will be required* −"

"Welcome, beloved, welcome!" Günther broke in hoarsely. I flinched and faltered.

"Louder, for God's sake!" Eglofstein whispered in my ear. "Louder, in heaven's name!"

"*How many cannon will be required to defend it adequately?*" My voice rose almost to a shout, and the words on the paper danced a fandango before my eyes. "*Does it have water, large open spaces, substantial buildings? Will it lend itself to the construction of depots, bakehouses, storehouses* −"

"Louder, Jochberg!" Eglofstein exclaimed. "I cannot understand a word!"

"– *storehouses for victuals*," I cried desperately, "*and an arsenal for ammunition. Last but not least, is there sufficient space to accommodate the baggage of an army corps? Kindly ascertain, Colonel, whether the town fulfils our requirements in the aforementioned respects . . .*" I broke off. "The next few lines are smudged, Captain."

"Leave that letter and proceed to the next."

I unfolded it, but the paper slipped through my fingers and fluttered to the floor. While stooping to retrieve it I heard Günther's voice once more, this time filled with reproach.

"I have implored you, dearest, to visit me now and then. Did he forbid you to leave the house? Ah, you obey his every last command . . ."

Those words could only be addressed to her – to Françoise-Marie! The colonel's face stiffened and Eglofstein went white to the lips. I snatched up the letter and read it out so wildly, so frantically and desperately, that Donop, who had just entered the room, stopped short, open-mouthed and unable to grasp what was afoot.

"*Colonel! The 25th Regiment of Chasseurs, which forms part of my division, has one hundred and fifty unmounted troopers at its cavalry depot. You should find it easy, in your part of the country, to remount those men by purchasing horses at moderate prices. Kindly make it your business to see that the regiment, which can muster only five hundred chargers in all, acquires another hundred remounts –*"

"But that was done long ago!" Donop called from the doorway. "I myself –"

"Be silent!" Eglofstein told him furiously. "Proceed, Jochberg. What next?"

"Letter dated 18th December and signed by Marshal Soult himself: *Colonel! The reports I have received from Vizcaya are such as to preclude my detaching a single man from there. The enemy is so intent on –*"

I paused for breath, and in the very same moment I heard Günther utter my name.

"You!" he hissed. "Was it Jochberg taught you that new lover's trick? Was it Donop? Answer me!"

"*The enemy is so intent on besieging the town,*" I bellowed, "*that he has, in the past two months, constructed a growing number of large magazines in the vicinity."*

"Next!" cried Eglofstein.

"Letter dated 22nd December from Colonel Desnuettes, Chief of Staff: *Colonel! I know as well as anyone how much it would redound to the Emperor's glory and advantage to proceed against Lord Wellington rather than against the rebel bands you mention. I cannot, however, advise the Marshal to grant your request, for I do not know –"*

"What was it Desnuettes wrote?" the colonel broke in, his interest suddenly aroused. "'Cannot advise' – was that it?"

"*Cannot, however, advise the Marshal to grant your request,*" I repeated. "He goes on: *for I do not know what threat we may expect from Asturias in the coming winter. Moreover, I am too short of first-rate infantry to enable me to approve –*"

"Stop!" the colonel burst out angrily. "What did you say: 'to approve'? Who is this Desnuettes to approve or recommend anything at all? His rank is no higher than mine. Eglofstein! Has this impudent communication been answered?"

"Not yet, Colonel."

"Take pen and paper. Write what I dictate and send it off at the first opportunity. I'll show Desnuettes!"

He strode angrily up and down the room. "Write as follows," he said. "*Colonel! Henceforward, confine your good offices to transmitting my suggestions to the Marshal unaccompanied by any form of recommendation, and kindly inform me of his –* No, that's not strong enough."

He had paused for thought and was silently moving his lips. I waited willy-nilly, unable to read on and uncertain what to do next. It was then, at the height of that breathless hush, that Günther spoke in his delirium – slowly, loudly, and with perfect clarity.

"Sweetheart," he said, "your blue buttercup – let me kiss it."

I do not know what went on inside me at that moment. Was I dazed, or did a hundred dreadful visions flash through my head and promptly vanish into oblivion? I only know that, when I recovered my wits, the shock of the foregoing seconds lingered in the form of trembling hands and an ice-cold rivulet trickling down my spine. And then I collected my thoughts. The moment had come at last – the moment we had dreaded for a twelvemonth – but I commanded myself to take heart and stand firm. I plucked up my courage and looked at the colonel.

He was standing erect and motionless, his mouth a little twisted as if the migraine were upon him. He continued to stand like that for a while. Then, with a sudden movement, he turned to Eglofstein. The storm, I felt sure, was about to break.

Quite calmly and serenely – almost placidly – he said, "Where was I? Ah yes, Eglofstein, take this down: *You would do well, Colonel, to confine yourself henceforward . . .*"

Was I dreaming? Was it possible? We had stolen his wife, he knew that now, yet he calmly continued to dictate his letter as if nothing untoward had happened. We all stared at him. Eglofstein sat there quill in hand, too stunned to write. Günther's voice impinged on the silence for a second time.

"The blue buttercup, do you hear?" he said. "Has Donop kissed it too, and Eglofstein, and Jochberg?"

Not a muscle of the colonel's face moved. He stood there in the watchful attitude of one listening, his lips a trifle pursed with sorrow or scorn. Then he turned abruptly toward the window. I now heard a distant sound from the street, a low hum, and he seemed to have ears for that alone.

Eglofstein rose with sudden decision. He flung down his quill, marched over to the colonel, and came to attention.

"Colonel," he said, straight as a ramrod, "I plead guilty. You may deal with me as you think fit, that goes without saying. I await your orders."

The colonel raised his head and looked at Eglofstein.

"My orders? The situation is too grave, I feel, to justify my depriving the regiment of even one of its officers for the sake of a mere bagatelle."

"A bagatelle?" Eglofstein said haltingly, returning the colonel's gaze.

A shrug. A careless wave of the hand.

"I was concerned to discover the truth, and now I know it. It fails to surprise me. The matter is over and done with."

I myself was numb with surprise and incomprehension. I had expected an outburst of fury, a passionate desire to destroy us all, only to be met with remarks that sounded cool and indifferent, almost philosophical.

When none of us spoke, the colonel went on, "I never cherished the illusion that the resemblance to which my senses succumbed was anything but superficial in the extreme. Face and deportment and colour of hair – yes, all those I found combined in her by some quirk of nature, but I never expected such a poor simulacrum to be faithful as well."

The din outside had grown louder and come closer, so much so that I could already pick out individual voices. Günther was still mumbling to himself, but none of us heeded his words.

"Why do you all look so puzzled?" said the colonel. "Did you seriously expect me to play the jealous pantaloon for the sake of a creature who has, I gather, made herself agreeable to every last one of you? A grand scene on account of such a trifle? Really, Eglofstein, I find you somewhat ridiculous at this moment. Now go and see what's up out there."

Eglofstein went to the window, threw both casements wide, and leaned out. I heard a confused hubbub. Then the din subsided. A gust of wind swept through the room, scattering the papers on the desk. Eglofstein came back.

"The mob broke through the cordon in the marketplace," he reported. "Lieutenant Lohwasser was dragged off his horse and mishandled."

"While we stand here arguing over women and affairs of the heart," exclaimed the colonel. "Come, Eglofstein!"

They snatched up their sabres and cloaks and hurried out, but a few seconds later Eglofstein returned alone.

"I'm pressed for time," he said quickly. "She must go, do you hear? He must not find her here on his return."

"Who must go?" asked Donop.

"Monjita."

"Monjita? Was it really she of whom he spoke?"

"Who else, in God's name? Do you imagine that any of us would have left this room alive had he guessed the truth? He never for a moment suspected that his wife had deceived him."

"And the blue buttercup?"

"Are you still groping in the dark?" Eglofstein said impatiently. "I saw you both standing there like dumb oxen. It dawned on me at once: he must have completed the illusion by etching the blue buttercup into Monjita's flesh, it's as plain as a pikestaff!"

"Mount up!" came the colonel's voice from below, followed by a clank of sabres and a jingle of spurs and accoutrements.

"She must go – now do you understand? He must never see her again or he'll learn the truth."

"But where shall she go?"

"That's your business. Out of this house – out of this town. I cannot stay."

He strode out. There was a minute's silence. Then I heard the multitudinous clatter of horses' hoofs receding in the direction of the marketplace.

THE FINAL SIGNAL

We found Monjita on the stairs. She was leaning against the bannisters staring blankly, listlessly, into space. She started at our approach, and we saw that her eyes were swimming with tears.

We both guessed at once from her distracted expression that she had encountered the colonel as he was leaving the house. Whatever it was that had so distressed her – a scornful remark, a hostile glance, a contemptuous gesture of dismissal, or merely the look on his face – she stood there helpless and despairing, at a loss to account for her lover's changed demeanour.

Donop went up to her and announced that she must leave the house. He had, he said, been ordered to take her to a place of greater safety, for it was feared that the town would be bombarded afresh when darkness fell.

Monjita might not have heard a word of what he told her.

"What's amiss?" she cried. "He was angry – angrier than I have ever seen him. Where has he gone? When will he return?"

Donop urged her to trust him and come with us. It would, he said, be foolish and dangerous to remain where she was.

Monjita fixed him with an uncomprehending gaze. Then, quite suddenly, her dismay turned to anger.

"You must have told the colonel that you met the tailor's son at my father's house – it must have been you or one of your friends. You did wrong, sir, for now he thinks the worst of me."

Knowing nothing of this "tailor's son", we stared at her in surprise.

"This much is true and the colonel knows it," she went on. "I did have a lover, but I have shunned him these last six months or more. It was through no fault of mine that I met him yesterday in my father's work-room. He had offered to impersonate Joseph of Arimathea for a real-and-a-half, but he did so only in order to see me. This morning, when I went to the window, he was loitering in the street below. He waved to me, but I ignored him. That's all there is to tell. Take me to the colonel – I'll convince him that I've done nothing wrong."

"The colonel is inspecting our forward positions," Donop said, abashed. "He will remain there all night – tomorrow as well, perhaps."

"Take me to him!" Monjita entreated. "Tell me how I can get to him and God will reward you both with a thousand years of bliss."

Donop glanced at me briefly. We felt ashamed that the unjust course of action on which we were embarked should have compelled us to lie and confirm Monjita in her misapprehension, but we had no choice. The colonel could never be permitted to see her again.

"Very well," said Donop, "please yourself, but the outposts are a long way off and well within range of the enemy's guns."

"No matter," Monjita cried joyfully. "I'll swim the river if I must."

But all at once mistrust took hold of her, or so it seemed, perhaps because she remembered how we had pestered her to spend the night with us. She looked long and searchingly, first at Donop, then at me, as if she feared we still had designs on her.

"Wait here for me," she said. "I must go upstairs to fetch some things for the night. I shall not be long."

She returned after a while, bearing a small bundle. When I offered to carry it for her, she surrendered it with a hint of reluctance.

It was light – so light that I scarcely felt its weight. I held it in my hand, unaware that what I carried was perdition itself.

163

That little bundle spelled our inexorable doom and the destruction of the regiment: it contained the final signal.

I had arranged with Donop that I should guide Monjita through our lines and escort her to an enemy outpost. Attached to all guerrilla bands were British staff officers dispatched by Wellington and Rowland Hill to advise their commanders on all matters relating to the art of warfare. I intended to parley with one of them under a flag of truce and entrust Monjita to his care, representing her as a lady of quality for whom the commander of the beleaguered garrison solicited the enemy's protection.

I had resolved to row up the river in a boat, for all that I had seen during my early morning sortie persuaded me that this would be the safest route. Moreover, should the guerrillas decline to respect a flag of truce, I would have some prospect of getting out of range at speed by using the current and keeping to the shelter of the bushes on the bank.

We boarded the skiff at a spot below the walls where the town's many washerwomen ordinarily plied their trade. I took the oars while Monjita crouched in the bottom of the boat with her bundle.

Shots could be heard from the vicinity of the marketplace – an ominous sign. Fighting was in progress against the insurgents, and it must have proved difficult to quell them, for the colonel would not otherwise have given the order to open fire. Darkness was falling when Donop took leave of me with a handshake. His expression conveyed doubt and concern, together with the fear that we would never meet again, for my mission was fraught with danger and far from assured of success.

A moist wind smote my cheeks as I slowly and silently dipped the oars and the river scents rose around me. Carried downstream by the current, large ice-floes and clumps of uprooted brushwood and reeds grazed the sides of the boat. I had to duck my head at times to avoid being struck by the willows whose naked branches reached far out across the water. In the distance, the river and the dusky outlines of the bushes that flanked it merged into one immense nocturnal shadow.

One of our pickets challenged me at the first bend. I put in to the bank. First-Lieutenant von Froben appeared, recognized me – much to his surprise – and inquired my purpose and destination. I told him no more than I deemed necessary.

I learned that our outworks were only sparsely manned, the bulk of the troops having retired within the walls. The revolt had assumed dangerous proportions, and the colonel was being hard-pressed by large numbers of insurgents in the centre of the town.

"Let's hope the guerrillas leave us in peace tonight," Froben added anxiously, peering through the darkness at the valley where Saracho's men lay encamped.

Monjita understood no word of our conversation save one: the colonel's name. At that she raised her head and looked at me inquiringly. I rowed on.

"Will we be there soon?" she asked.

"Soon enough," I replied.

"But where are you taking me?" she said, growing uneasy. "Look, I can see the camp-fires of the Serranos." (The Spanish townsfolk called the guerrillas Serranos or "highlanders".)

I thought it time to tell her the truth.

"I have brought you here, Monjita, to place you under the protection of an enemy officer."

She gave a faint cry of surprise and consternation.

"And the colonel?"

"You will never see him again."

She stood up, causing the skiff to rock violently.

"You deceived me!" she cried, so close that I could feel her breath on my cheek.

"I had no choice. You'll resign yourself in the end, I'm sure. I have the highest opinion of your intelligence."

"Take me back or I'll call for help!"

"Do so by all means, but you'll call in vain. The sentries will not let you past the gate."

Despairingly, she broke into a flood of threats, entreaties and lamentations, but I stood firm. An idea had taken root in my mind: by carrying off Monjita in my skiff, I was lifting a curse from the regiment and the town. It was for her sake that we had given Bolibar's first and second signals, just as it was her fault that we had quarrelled with Günther, and that he now lay dead or dying in Eglofstein's room. If she saw the colonel again, she could not fail – to his detriment and ours – to disclose the true nature of our secret.

She ceased to plead and lament when she saw that it was futile, and I heard her quietly praying. Sobs mingled with her fervent supplications. Then she fell silent and I heard nothing more from her, just a gentle sigh and a low, lingering moan.

By now I had come to the second bend in the river. Great heaps of brushwood blazing on either bank turned its entire surface into a watery inferno of colour. Shadows flitted hither and thither on the shore. Then a voice hailed me, a shot rang out, and a bullet struck the water close beside my skiff.

I let go of the oars, hurriedly lit the lantern at my feet in the bottom of the boat, and swung it to and fro with one hand while waving a white handkerchief with the other. The skiff drifted into the bank. Guerrillas came running from all sides with lanterns, hurricane lamps and torches. There were now more than a hundred of them awaiting me at the water's edge, and among them, to my joy, I saw the scarlet cloak and white panache of a British officer in the Northumberland Fusiliers.

I leapt ashore with the handkerchief held high, strode up to this officer without heeding the others, and, with a dozen musket barrels levelled at my head, explained the reason for my presence.

He listened to me in silence, then made for Monjita, presumably intending to help her out of the skiff. I was about to follow when I felt a hand grip my shoulder and turned to find myself confronted by Colonel Saracho.

I recognized the Tanner's Tub at once. He was leaning on a stick, his massive legs swathed in strips of rag. Stuck in his red sash were knives, cartridges, pistols, several heads of garlic, and a lump of bread. Around his neck he wore a thong arrayed on which, like rosary beads, were pieces of biscuit.

"First and foremost," he growled, "you're my prisoner. As to the rest, we shall see."

"I came under a flag of truce," I protested.

Saracho chuckled gleefully.

"You drifted ashore like a rotting fish," he said. "And now, surrender your sword."

I hesitated, gauging the distance between the skiff and the spot where I stood. Before I could act, however, the British officer came over to me.

"Your commanding officer sends strange gifts," he drawled. "That girl is dead."

"Dead?" I exclaimed, and darted toward the skiff. Quick as I was, Saracho got there first. He bent over Monjita and shone his lantern on her face.

"She's dead, sure enough," he croaked. "What are we to do with her? Did you bring her here that we should sing a *Miserere* for her, say an Office for the Dead, a *De profundis*, a *Requiescat*, a rosary?"

Before I could reply he gave a startled exclamation like the snarl of an infuriated cat. Straightening up, he gave me a long, hard stare.

"So that's it," he said in an altogether different tone of voice. "The knife has returned to its owner, eh? Very well, mark this!"

He drew a double-barrelled pistol from his sash. I reached for my sabre, thinking it was meant for me, but he fired both barrels in the air, one after the other, and whistled shrilly betweentimes.

I knew that guerrilla's signal: it was a call to arms.

Saracho's bulky frame was still obstructing my view of the skiff and Monjita, but all at once I caught sight of his right hand. It was holding the dagger whose ivory hilt bore a representation of the Virgin with Christ's corpse across her knees: Bolibar's third signal!

The ground lurched beneath my feet. The men, the torches, the trees around me slowly swayed and revolved. My eyes discerned nothing but the knife and the drop of blood adhering to it: a drop of Monjita's life-blood. They followed that drop

167

as it trickled down the blade, slowly, steadily and relentlessly, as if in obedience to some terrible, irrevocable law. And all at once I saw Monjita before me as I had seen her for the very first time. "Come here, you of the burning eyes!" The colonel's words rang in my head, and there she stood beside his armchair with the firelight upon her, and an infinity of sorrow and despair overcame me at the thought that she was dead. But now a voice cried out within me – a stranger's voice, not my own.

"That was the third signal!" it cried with angry vehemence. "The third signal, and you gave it!"

Then another voice spoke, seemingly from a great way off. I awoke from my dreamlike state to find myself alone on the river bank with Saracho and the British captain.

"Inform the one who sent you," the Tanner's Tub was saying, "that a quarter of an hour from now . . ." He broke off. "It's you, by all the saints and angels! Or is it? This time I'm truly unsure."

He drew back, held his lantern close to my face, and began to laugh.

"It seems to me I saw this gentleman only lately, wearing morocco shoes and silken hose. How say you, Captain?"

The British officer smiled.

"It delights me to recognize you despite your disguise, My Lord Marquis. As I have had the honour to assure you once before, sir, yours is not a face one readily forgets."

"The Señor Marques has done his work well," Saracho growled contentedly. "If the townsfolk have risen in revolt, La Bisbal is as good as ours. We shall storm it a quarter of an hour from now."

And the singular thing was that in me, Lieutenant Jochberg of the Nassau Grenadiers, those words aroused the feeling that I was indeed the Marquis of Bolibar, and for the space of a second I experienced *his* pride and exultation at having given the third signal and completed *his* task.

And then that momentary delusion left me: I recovered my wits and became my wretched, despairing self again.

168

Transfixed with horror, I knew that I must return at once, warn my comrades, raise the alarm . . .

I was into the skiff in a trice.

"Where are you off to?" the British captain called after me. "Stay here with us, your work is done!"

"Not yet!" I cried, and the skiff, aided by the current, sped downstream.

CATASTROPHE

My memory has retained but little, thank heaven, of those doom-laden hours in which the Nassau Regiment and the Crown Prince's Own fought their last terrible and unavailing battle. The events of that last night have become compressed in my mind into a shadowy phantasmagoria of fire and blood, whirling snow and clouds of powder-smoke. Captain von Eglofstein I never saw again. As for Brockendorf, he appeared to me only in a dream. One rainy night at home in Germany many years later, I was abruptly wakened by a nightmare. I had seen Brockendorf – seen him quite plainly in my sleep as he burst from a blazing house with four Spaniards in pursuit. He wore neither shirt nor tunic, and I could see the curly black hairs on his barrel of a chest. He was wielding his sabre with one hand and fending off sword-thrusts with the other, which had his cloak wound round it. Three or four blows he delivered; then he dropped his sabre and fell to the ground. A small, fat, bearded man carrying a lantern bent over him and took possession of the cloak.

While the little bearded fellow was inspecting his prize and weighing it in his hand, there came a shot – a shot that made no sound – and he collapsed with Brockendorf's cloak draped over him. A full moon slowly emerged from behind the clouds, and the wind buried both corpses beneath a mound of driven snow.

Was it only a nocturnal hallucination, a belated nightmare, that wrested me from my uneasy slumbers, or did I really witness Brockendorf's death, and had the tumult of the time so completely erased that spectacle from my mind, like so many others, that I forgot it until a distressing dream retrieved it from the depths of oblivion many years after the event? I cannot say.

I did, however, see the colonel fall with my own eyes, as well as Donop and the rest, because I came too late to warn them: the third signal and Saracho's assault sealed their fate.

I leapt ashore and burst through the willows on the bank to find myself among some fleeing grenadiers who had abandoned our forward positions. The guerrillas were hot on their heels and gave them no respite. Each man ran for his life, though many fell, never to rise again. Swept along by the turmoil, I came at last to the outskirts of the town.

Here I overtook First-Lieutenant von Froben, who had been badly wounded and was reeling along the wall of a house like a drunken man. I eventually managed to persuade a handful of the fugitives to make a stand, and for a while we held the guerrillas off. Then came a sudden rumour that the rebels had outflanked us and were firing on us from the rear. There was no holding the men after that. They jumped up and fled down the street, and I with them.

Panic and confusion reigned on all sides. Everyone jostled and yelled and shoved. Bricks, earthenware pitchers, billets of firewood, iron implements, shingles, spits, tin cans, cooking pots and empty bottles rained down on our heads from every window. In the entrance of one house, at the top of some stairs leading down to the cellar, a young woman big with child stood firing a double-barrelled pistol into the street, reloading again and again. A man beside me paused and took aim at her. Then the moon disappeared behind the clouds and I saw no more. We ran on in the gloom, hearing cries of encouragement and despair all around us.

"My horse has gone! Where's my horse?"

"Courage, men! Wait till they come within range!"

"Where to, where to? All I can see is snow."

"Dragoons! Sons of France! Stand fast and club your carbines!"

"My knapsack!"

"On your feet, man! Pull yourself together, we must press on!"

"Ready, aim, fire!"

"Here I am, over here!"

"I'm hit, I can't go on."

"They're coming!"

"Forward, forward!"

Someone knocked me to the ground. All I felt for a moment was wet snow against my face and a stabbing pain in the back of the head. What happened to me then I cannot recall. Although I did not lose consciousness for an instant, my recollection of the next few minutes is a dark void.

When I came to myself I was being half supported, half dragged along by two grenadiers. I felt thirsty. My left arm was aching badly, as were my head and both shoulders. I fired my pistol twice, but at whom I cannot remember.

There were seven of us. All but two had discarded their weapons and nearly all were wounded.

And then we came in sight of the marketplace, which was brightly lit and thronged with men. We shouted for joy and embraced each other, thinking ourselves safe at last, when we found it held by three companies of grenadiers drawn up in defensive squares with the colonel sitting his horse in their midst.

It seemed that the regiment had been split in three at the very outset of the fighting. One group held out for a while near the presbytery and another took cover behind the trees and hedges of the hospital garden, which was later stormed by guerrillas and insurgent townsfolk. The three companies in the marketplace were still in good shape, however, and the plan was that we should try to fight our way through to the river.

Only snatches of the ensuing battle linger in my memory. Donop was standing beside me at one point. He spoke to me and offered me a drink from his canteen. Later I remember kneeling behind a baggage waggon, firing my carbine into a close-packed mass of attackers while a grenadier beside me drank cold soup from an earthenware bowl.

I could see the windows of my billet from where I knelt. They

172

were lit up, and I glimpsed the shadowy forms of unknown intruders flitting to and fro behind them. It occurred to me as I pulled the trigger that I had left some books lying on my table – French romances and a volume of German pasquinades.

The air was filled with a symphony of hisses, roars and whistles, rattling musketry, shrill screams, shouted orders, and the Spaniards' incessant *"Caraxo! Caraxo!"* Castel-Borckenstein was carried past me unconscious with blood welling from his boots. His servant followed behind, angrily shaking his empty musket at the enemy. Across the way, brightly illumined by torchlight outside the door of the "Blood of Christ" inn, St Antony held his stone arms aloft and continued to testify, amid the din and pother of battle, that Mary's conception was immaculate.

Immediately after Castel-Borckenstein was wounded came the order to retire. A half-company led the way in close order along the Calle Ambrosio with the colonel bringing up the rear.

Suddenly I saw him sway in the saddle. Two men sprang to his aid and held him up. He was past speaking, it seemed, but he gestured fiercely in the direction of the guerrillas. I lost sight of him in the press soon afterward. Donop called loudly, two or three times, for a litter.

All discipline was lost from then on. I was swept along by a tide of humanity and found myself in the Calle Geronimo, which seethed with running, shouting men, all striving to be the first to reach the bridge and the river bank. For some reason I never discovered, most of them later turned about and ran back again. Donop was still close beside me. While running – such is the picture of him I preserve to this day – he staunched a sabre-cut on his cheek with a piece of cloth torn from the lining of his tunic.

I dimly recall a brief mêlée near the nailsmith's forge, which had been destroyed by fire. Another of my memories is of a cascade of boiling water that landed just short of my feet. A few drops splashed my hand.

We found, when we came to the river, that the guerrillas had occupied the bridge. Some of our men tried to reach the farther bank by wading and swimming. They fought the current shoulder-deep, but the icy water numbed their limbs and they sank below the surface one by one. Meanwhile, the guerrillas poured case-shot into our ranks from the bridge.

We ran back the way we had come, keeping close to the walls. None of us now had any thought of safety or escape. There was neither hope nor despair in our hearts, just a mute determination to defend ourselves to the last. We sought no way out of our predicament, merely a spot where we could fight to the death bare-handed, man against man.

We entered a steep, narrow street in which I had never set foot before. This was where Donop fell. I made to help him up, thinking that he had slipped on the frozen ground, but a musket ball had lodged in his throat. He reached for my hand and gave me all his belongings: a silver fob-watch, two packets of letters, two bank-notes, a few gold Napoleons, a translation of Suetonius which he himself had begun, a small silver tablet adorned with mythological figures in relief, and a half-empty bottle of wine. A grenadier stooping under the weight of his pack, to which he had tied his boots, a copper kettle and a silver punch-bowl, interrupted his flight long enough to cast a covetous glance at the coins in my hand. I pocketed the things Donop had given me, but most of them I lost within minutes. All that I still have today is the little silver tablet portraying Venus and the Hours.

While hurrying on we heard a shrill whistle, which was answered from two directions. Almost simultaneously, we came under fire from our front. We halted and looked around in search of cover.

The door of the house beside us was quickly broken down with a musket butt. Beyond it lay a winding wooden staircase dimly lit by an oil-lamp burning in a niche below the image of some saint or other. The room at the head of the stairs appeared to be the store-room of a baker or confectioner. It contained sacks of flour, baskets filled with chestnuts and walnuts, a barrel of eggs packed in oaten straw, and a box of chocolate with the words "Pantin, rue Saint-Anne à Marseille" inscribed in black on the lid.

We left the door open, loaded our carbines, and took cover behind a stout table. We did not have long to wait, for footsteps could already be heard on the stairs.

A head came into view – a bony face surmounted by short, bristly hair. I recognized it at once as belonging to the spice merchant on the corner of the Calle de los Carmelitas. I raised my pistol, but someone behind me was quicker and fired first. Other figures appeared and rushed at us, shots rang out, an axe came hurtling across the table, powder-smoke filled the room.

We were alone when the air cleared, but only four of us were still standing. Our attackers could be heard blundering and tumbling down the stairs. We reloaded all our fire-arms including those of the two dead and laid them ready on the table in front of us.

One of the grenadiers, who reminded me that we had been schoolfellows years ago, begged a pinch of snuff. Another, too footsore to run any further, pulled his boots off. I myself was dropping with fatigue.

Then they came a second time.

A bullet whistled past my ear and something crashed to the ground behind me. Curses and shouts rent the air, two hands gripped my throat, and I was hurled to the floor.

"Make way!" a voice called from the door as I fell. Poised above me was an upraised sword. It hovered there for an eternity – hovered but did not descend.

"Stand aside, I say!" It was the same voice. Someone shone a lantern on my face, dazzling me. The sword disappeared, and in its place I saw a white panache and a scarlet cloak.

The hands slowly detached themselves from my throat. My head fell back and struck the edge of a crate.

"What madness to remain in that disguise," said the voice in my ear, then: "Pick him up! Carry him downstairs!"

I felt myself hoisted into the air.

"I warned you, did I not?" I heard. "There was always a danger that my men would fail to recognize you."

I tried to open my eyes, but it was no use. The wind struck cold and damp on my cheeks. Someone spread a cloak over me. I felt a rocking, swaying motion, and it seemed to me that

I was on the river again, sitting in the skiff with Monjita while the current sent ice-floes bumping along the sides and willow trees rustled on the bank.

Then all was still. The rocking sensation ceased, and I was bedded down on something soft.

"Who the devil is that, Captain?" asked a gruff, surly voice.

"The Marquis of Bolibar," came the reply.

Another beam of light on my face, whispers, muffled footsteps. The footsteps grew fainter and a door closed.

I fell asleep.

THE MARQUIS OF BOLIBAR

It was late in the day when I awoke.

Still dazed with sleep and unable to open my eyes, I had a vague feeling that the room where I lay was thronged with people standing shoulder to shoulder and watching me in silence. By the time I was fully awake, the last three were tiptoeing out, each gesturing to the others to tread softly and steal away without a sound.

Only two men remained: the captain in the Northumberland Fusiliers, who stood over my bed in his scarlet cloak, arms folded, and, seated beside the fire, Colonel Saracho.

As soon as I saw the latter, the events of the previous day, which sleep had suffered me to forget, came flooding back: the guerrillas' onslaught, the deaths of the colonel and Donop and Castel-Borckenstein, the annihilation of both regiments. Boundless amazement overcame me that I should still be alive, followed at once by a numbing pang of terror that one of the men confronting me should be my mortal foe, the Tanner's Tub. An instant later, however, my fear was displaced by a profoundly soothing thought: as the last survivor of the regiment I had no right to go on living, and what better fate could I wish for than to join my comrades in the grave?

"He's awake," I heard the British officer say.

Saracho gave a hoarse exclamation that sounded like a groan. Clearly visible in the firelight, his legs were stretched out on a chair and thickly swathed in rags on account of the podagra from which he had suffered for years. His left arm was bandaged from elbow to shoulder.

"My respects, Señor Marques," he grunted as he scratched one gouty ankle. "How is Your Excellency feeling?"

I stared at him, convinced that he was making mock of me.

"Finding you was no easy matter," the British captain reported. "It was only pure chance, My Lord Marquis, that granted me the honour of escorting you to safety."

I sprang to my feet. Destiny had chosen the strangest way of saving my life, I saw that now. A shiver ran down my spine at the thought that I should have been cast in the role of one whom I had helped to murder, and I resolved to end the grisly masquerade at once.

"I am not the man you take me for," I told the captain, forcing myself to look him in the eye. "The Marquis of Bolibar is long dead. I am a German officer in the service of the Confederation of the Rhine."

Having made this avowal, I awaited my fate with an easy mind.

The Britisher looked first at Saracho and then at me.

"Ah yes," he said with a smile, "I know: the same German officer who presented himself at Your Lordship's country seat some days ago, just half an hour after you disappeared – a strange coincidence of which I was apprised by your steward, Fabricio. He came here this morning while you slept."

"Damnation," Saracho interjected, "I've a nail-maker's smithy in these legs of mine – no one would believe how they prick and twinge."

"You're mistaken, Captain," I exclaimed. "I am Lieutenant Jochberg of the Nassau Regiment."

"Late of the Nassau Regiment, yes, My Lord Marquis, and the strangest by far of all the soldiers in the Emperor's service."

"Soldiers, you call them?" Saracho cried angrily. He made to rise, only to sink back in his chair with an anguished groan. "Soldiers, did you say? Libertines, more like – lechers and braggarts, gamblers and drunkards, liars and gluttons, despoilers of churches. God is just and his retribution well-merited!"

I was overcome with grief and rage when I heard my dead comrades reviled in this way. I started toward Saracho, intending to throttle him with my bare hands, but the British officer barred my path.

"So you take me for the Marquis of Bolibar," I said, when I had regained my composure. "Why? The Marquis was an elderly man, whereas I am only eighteen years old."

Saracho gave a bleating laugh.

"Eighteen, eh? A fine age, to be sure. The candle-maker across the way from the church – you knew him, Señor Marques, he was so thin he might have been sired by a ramrod – well, that man was fifty years old when he took his third wife, and for the wedding he dyed his hair as handsome a brown as yours was yesterday. *He* looked eighteen too, but not for long. A pity you wasted all that goat's grease, pomade and beeswax, Señor Marques. It hasn't lasted longer than a night."

He laughed again and pointed to a broken mirror on the wall. I caught sight of my reflection and blenched, unable to believe my eyes: the terrible events of the previous night had turned my hair white – snow-white, like that of an old man.

"You do wrong, My Lord Marquis," said the captain's voice in my ear. "You do wrong to try to flee the world in that disguise. You played your part in a great and noble venture. Heaven was with you, so it succeeded. You should not belittle that glorious deed. You should not disdain the gratitude owed you by us all – by your native land and the cause of freedom."

I do not know how it came about, that mysterious phenomenon, but I no longer saw myself as I stood gazing into the mirror: I saw a strange old man with white hair. And then, in some weird and inexplicable way, I felt his thoughts awaken within me. His prowess, his determination, his resolve came alive and took possession of me. I experienced a fierce thrill of elation. It was as if the soul of the murdered man had got to grips with my own, the soul of his murderer, and was striving to oust it. The Marquis of Bolibar, great and terrible man that he was, had invaded my body. I tried to fight him off, tried to repossess myself, tried to conjure up the faces of my dead

179

comrades, forced myself to think of them – of Donop, Eglofstein and Brockendorf – but they refused to emerge from the darkness. I had forgotten the sound of their voices, and when my own inner voice tried to call their names aloud the words that rose to my lips were those of a stranger: Saracho's cruel words had become mine.

"Braggarts and gluttons, drunkards and despoilers of churches," cried the voice within me. "God is just and his retribution well-merited."

And I felt as if the regiments' destruction had been my own desire from the first – as if I had willed it on behalf of a great and noble cause. A tempest shook me, my heart pounded, my temples throbbed, and I swayed, overwhelmed by the grandeur of the moment.

Saracho expected me to speak, from the look on his face, but I remained silent.

"Let me tell you something, Señor Marques," he began. "I know that you despise war and think little of the glory won in battle by a gallant soldier. The humble peasant who innocently tills his field is far more glorious than any general or marshal – wasn't that how you put it? Well, I pondered on all manner of things last night, being unable to sleep for pain. A shell splinter gashed my arm, and if gangrene sets in . . ." He shrugged. "But that's by the by. My point is that we soldiers are martyrs quite as much as St James, or St Cyriac, or St Marcellinus – martyrs of God or the Devil, who knows? What do we fight for? What do we bleed for? For God's sake? Being blind, earth-bound moles, one and all, we cannot know God's true purpose. To fill our own pockets? Señor Marques, we soldiers are like Noah's carpenters, who built the Ark for all living things and were afterward drowned themselves. For the welfare of our country? This soil, Señor Marques, has drunk a deal of blood in the last thousand years, and who cares today about a battle fought a hundred years ago? So why all the fighting, the marching, the hardships, the hunger, the danger, the wounds? What remains of all those things? I'll tell you, Señor Marques: what remains is glory! I walk through the streets of a strange town and men whisper my name behind my back, mothers hold their children aloft, townsfolk run out of their houses and faces are pressed to windows. And one day, when I am old and weary and crawl on all fours into some monastery, the glory associated with my name will still endure. I'm one of the Devil's own, God help me!"

He fell silent. A hideous old hag had entered the room bearing a bowl of warm water and a piece of rag. The British captain took his plumed shako from the table and made off as soon as he saw her.

"You fool, you booby, you good-for-nothing!" she snarled as she proceeded to bathe Saracho's wounded arm. "Look at you sitting there, groaning! Other men go in quest of gold; two ounces of lead is all you ever bring home!"

"Gently, woman!" groaned the victim of her ministrations. "Leave me in peace – I've just won a famous victory."

"A famous victory?" the old woman squawked, brandishing her piece of rag. "To what purpose? None, save that the same king, and not some other, should levy fresh taxes on bread and dripping and cheese and eggs in the years to come!"

"Silence!" cried Saracho. "Wield your broom and stop meddling in my business! Don't you recognize His Excellency the Señor Marques?"

"Excellency and eminence and reverence and pestilence! Why must you always be in the thick of things? If the Turks set about the Tatars, *you* would insist on being there."

"Ah me," Saracho groaned, "I've had this millstone around my neck for seventeen long years. She grows worse every day. Her bile is only to be measured by the bucketful!"

"The whole town knows you for an idler," snapped the harridan. "You roam the countryside and think it would soil your hands to do some honest work for once."

"Lord," Saracho sighed, long and mournfully, "deliver me from all evil!"

I could still hear the guerrilla colonel's plaintive voice and his wife's vituperations when I left the room and made my way downstairs. Some rebel officers were sitting under a fig tree outside the house, devouring roast mutton. They silently rose to their feet as I passed.

The streets teemed with brisk, bustling figures. The townsfolk were eagerly going about their business, and there was no outward sign that the town had, only hours before, witnessed the death-throes of two regiments. Chestnut-sellers sat on their corkwood chairs, stall-keepers set out their wares, small carts laden with charcoal rattled through the streets, muleteers trotted their beasts to and fro for the benefit of would-be purchasers, barbers offered their services, a Carmelite friar distributed scapulars and holy pictures, and the cries of peasant women selling divers kinds of merchandise rang out on all sides:

"Milk! Goats' milk! Warm milk! Who'll buy?"

"Onions from Murcia! Nuts from Vizcaya! Garlic! Beans! Olives from Seville!"

"Wine! Red wine! Wine from Val de Peñas!"

"Sausages of every kind. *Salchichónes! Longanizas! Chorizos!* Genuine sausages from Estremadura!"

And, wherever I went, the noise and bustle died away. Hurrying townsfolk paused and stood aside to let me pass before staring after me with awe, amazement and mute admiration writ large on their faces.

It was the Marquis of Bolibar who walked the streets of his town, not I. I caught a distant glimpse of vineyards and fields, and a triumphant voice within me cried, "*My* land, *my* native soil! It is for me that those fields turn green and those vines bear fruit. All that this sky encompasses is mine!" I was a man transformed – I was heir to this alien land for the space of an hour. And so, with my heart aglow and my head filled with dreams, I made my way slowly out of La Bisbal.

A detachment of guerrillas was drawn up beside the town wall. One of them flung open the gates and saluted me with eyes downcast.

"*Ave Maria purissima!*" he cried, and the unfamiliar words that issued from my lips were uttered in a dead man's voice:

"Amen! She conceived without sin."